CW00794163

OUT OF REACH

Carolyn, never having seen her real father, decides to track him down, although she's devastated that her boyfriend, Andy, is against the scheme. Nevertheless, she sets out alone to Australia, meeting the attractive Nick Packer en route. Soon her quest to find her father seems impossible. Far from her home and family, her relationship with Andy becomes increasingly frosty, whilst her ripening friendship with Nick suddenly seems so very tempting ... Caroline has some serious choices to make.

BETH JAMES

◆

OUT OF
REACH

Complete and Unabridged

LINFORD
Leicester

First published in Great Britain in 2009

First Linford Edition
published 2010

British Library CIP Data

James, Beth.
   Out of reach.- -(Linford romance library)
   1. Birthfathers- -Fiction.
   2. Australia- -Fiction.
   3. Love stories.
   4. Large type books.
   I. Title II. Series
   823.9′2–dc22

   ISBN 978–1–44480–490–4

Published by
F. A. Thorpe (Publishing)
Anstey, Leicestershire

Set by Words & Graphics Ltd.
Anstey, Leicestershire
Printed and bound in Great Britain by
T. J. International Ltd., Padstow, Cornwall

This book is printed on acid-free paper

1

Trying not to panic I watched my travel bag lumber its way onto the conveyer belt and disappear from sight. Clutching my boarding pass in my hand and hitching my backpack-come-hand luggage more firmly on my shoulders, I thanked the smiling ground crew. I knew I'd reached the airport way too early but, trying to appear the seasoned traveller I most certainly was not, I threaded my way through the crowds to where I could watch the screen for my boarding gate number. I found a handy seat from where I could, at the same time, have a view for any late arrivals coming to see me off — maybe.

I smiled grimly to myself for there was no maybe about it. I'd bidden my friends farewell two days ago and my mother and stepfather a tearful 'goodbye' that morning. And Andy?

Well, I'd rather not think about Andy right now.

So why was I searching the crowds in desperation, just praying for a glimpse of his tall frame, his untidy hair and quiet, serious smile? It was sheer stupidity to watch for Andy's appearance when I'd been the very one to forbid him to come. Not that he would want to now — I'd surely seen to that.

A hot uncomfortable feeling stole over me as I remembered some of the unforgivable things I'd said on our last encounter. Why had I expected so much of him? Why had I assumed he'd understand? It seemed I'd been wrong about Andy when I'd thought he was special, that we were destined to be soul mates. There was nothing special about being uncompromising and stubborn and that was exactly what he was.

It was just as well he hadn't come to see me off really, I told myself on the edge of a tear, because we would only have quarrelled again. The last thing I wanted before I stepped on to my flight for Perth, Australia, was an embarrassing scene with my boyfriend. Sorry — my ex-boyfriend.

Resolving not to examine the crowds any longer, I bought myself a paper and a best seller. But despite my intention, as I leafed through the paper, full of celebrity gossip though it was, my mind refused to focus on the photos of the stars and their ever changing partners staring at me from the pages. Instead I saw Andy's tightly closed expression which failed to mask the hurt in his eyes, the last time I'd seen him.

'OK, Carolyn — if that's the way you want it,' he'd said eventually, and then he walked away. Just like that. I'd not even received a text from him, on my new mobile phone bought specially with Australia in mind. How final was that?

The number-filled screen clicked over. There it was, my departure gate was open. My stomach started to churn with a strange mixture of excitement and fear as I gathered my things together and headed for the departure gate.

The departure lounge when, after seemingly endless miles of carpet later, I reached it, seemed to be full of couples and families. I hoped I wasn't the only person to be travelling alone, although quite what difference that would make I couldn't have explained. Glancing at my watch for perhaps the millionth time, I wondered what it would be like, first in Singapore, although that was only for a two-hour break, then Perth.

It was early November and in London, a cold and dreary November at that. Now the fireworks had been and gone, the streets were full of grey-faced people with only Christmas then a miserable winter to look forward to. I was lucky to be heading for warmer climes I told myself, even if my reason for going was rather out of the ordinary and, to say the least — vague!

Before I knew it, I was part of a line of, fed up already, travellers queuing to board the plane. I wondered if mine was the only heart beating faster than normal as I made my way down the aisle towards my allocated seat.

I had only one piece of overhead baggage and was able to stow it away easily. There's very little room for manoeuvre in plane aisles and as I bent to retrieve my book and sweater from my seat, my bottom banged into someone impatiently trying to get past me in the aisle.

Trust me! I catapulted forward and somehow managed to land in my seat. 'Sorry,' I said. 'So sorry.' Then as I turned, my eyes met those of someone I recognised. I couldn't quite place where or when I'd seen him before, only knew that I had — and quite recently too. 'Hello there,' I said spontaneously. 'What are you doing here?'

The guy with whom I'd been playing hands, knees and bumps-a-daisies, totally ignored me. He stared down his superior looking nose and blanked me, before continuing his way down the aisle towards the back of the plane.

Right, fine! My face burned with annoyance as I turned quickly away. OK well, I wouldn't be doing too much smiling at anyone else then.

The other passengers in my row were all nicely settled so, without looking in the direction of Mr Familiar-but-Arrogant, who obviously didn't want to be known — not by me anyway, I attended diligently to what the flight attendant was saying.

Then I read my safety-in-board card, even though I knew it by heart, after which I shut my eyes and prepared to catch up on the sleep I had missed out on over the last couple of weeks.

But of course the thoughts still kept churning round in my brain. Was I truly, as Andy had said accusingly, setting off on a wild goose chase? Had I really not thought things through? My mother's words this time. Was I completely stark, staring, bonkers to throw up a well paid job that I loved and squander my savings, on a whim?

This was a little voice in the back of my brain, which nagged persistently in the small hours of the night.

Resolutely, I pushed all my doubts aside. This was something I had to do. Something I'd been putting off all my life, and I'd made the decision — it had to be now while I had no ties, no responsibilities and above all the courage and the reason.

Over twenty-two years I'd grown used to the fact that I'd never seen my real father. My mother had explained it to me simply and logically. 'Your father is a free spirit, Caro,' she told me. 'We loved each other — you were born. He loved you — make no mistake, but he was in the music business and his life was only just beginning to take off. He had the potential to make it big and he was set on conquering America. These showbiz marriages don't stand a chance. The kids grow up unsettled. The life of a roadie is no life for a child.'

'But why can't I see him?' I remember asking once. 'Just for a minute. I wouldn't be a nuisance, I promise.'

Mum had looked sad, but quickly put her arms round me for a cuddle. 'Darling, it's best this way. We were young; we wanted different things . . . No, it's worked out for the best. It would have been too hard any other way — believe me. We discussed it and in the end I gave him his freedom, and he gave me you!'

I suppose I must have been a fairly simple child because I accepted the situation. By that time my stepfather, Roger, was on the scene, I had learned to love him and trust him and call him Dad, and I was happy and caught up in my own little world. Other children had surnames different from their parents, and had stepfathers. Not all of them heard from their real father in the way that I did.

For every birthday I received a package — usually quite small, only a padded envelope, and inside would be what I came to regard as treasures. Sometimes it would be a small silver charm or a pretty ribbon. Maybe a book or a paper cut-out doll. There was nearly always money too.

Mum would click her tongue at sending so much through the post. Usually it was American or Australian dollars; once it was Euros, he must have been in Germany then, Mum said, because of the postmark. But although it was very carefully put away in my account, it wasn't the money I was interested in. Occasionally there was no money, only the gift of a pressed flower or a parrot's feather. Those times Mum looked worried. 'Hard times,' she'd say, 'poor old Brad.'

So one way or another, I'd got to thinking of my dad as some kind of long haired wandering minstrel. A guy who roamed the world in his shirt of many colours with a guitar strapped to his back and a wine glass in his hand on the wrist of which was a tattooed anchor. Just exactly how he was in the one faded photo Mum had of him.

'Brad knew his wines all right,' was

another thing I remember Mum saying. 'He used to swirl the drink around in the glass, stick his nose in and sniff. 'Ah, a hint of leather,' he'd say. 'Very loamy soil. Good year. Lots of sun.' Sometimes he'd even name the region. At first I thought he was kidding me, but when we looked at the label he was generally right. Didn't go with the rest of his lifestyle really — but there you are. He said once he'd done some grape-picking in France so perhaps that was it.'

With my head resting against the reclined seat of the plane, I smiled a bit as I reminisced on all this. As a teenager of course, I'd wanted to know more about this romantic shadowy figure that was my dad. Things I couldn't tell from the twenty-two year old photograph Mum had had copied for me. Things like what colour eyes did he have — blue the same as mine, and did he speak with an Australian accent — yes, but it was only slight . . .

When it came to my dad, there was

never a lot to go on, it was something I'd always accepted.

But this last September my twenty-second birthday had come and gone — and nothing arrived from my father. Watching Mum's expression change from bewildered and anxious, to sad and accepting, I let two whole months go by, but then I was determined to act.

'Perhaps he's decided you're grown up enough now not to expect birthday gifts,' she said in a voice that lacked conviction.

'Do you really believe that?' I asked because I knew that the one condition he'd made was that his daughter was aware that he was out there somewhere and he would send a gift on every birthday. And until now — he had.

Mum sighed. 'No Caro, not really . . . Perhaps he's hit hard times.'

'He's hit hard times before.' I was thinking of the mother of pearl shell collected off some deserted Australian beach, wrapped in a scrap of newspaper and a twice used padded envelope.

'He's always sent something — even if it was only a card and a poem — you know he has.'

Mum's eyes flickered away from mine.

'You think he's dead, don't you?'

'Darling . . . I don't know, but I'm very much afraid he might be — yes!'

There was a long silence during which I thought that surely I'd know, surely I'd feel something if my own father were dead.

I took a deep breath. 'Well, I have to find out.'

'Caro, your father was the love of my life. I love Roger, of course I do, but it's different. I had to let Brad go and it would have been too hard to stay in contact. If he'd stayed, his wonderful spirit would have been choked to death. We would have ended up hating each other. This way we kept our dream . . . We were young. Much, much too young.'

'You've told me all this before.'

Mum took a deep breath. 'I know

darling, but the other thing is . . . Caro, Brad's always had my address — it's partly why I've never moved from this house. But I have no contact address for him. I always thought that if he died he would have left provision for us to receive notification at least. But since your birthday I've been thinking that, perhaps like I have, he's made a new life for himself somewhere else and perhaps his new family don't need to know about us.'

I sat down rather suddenly. This was a thought that had never previously occurred to me.

'Well then it's even more imperative that I find out,' I said eventually. 'I . . . For goodness sake, I might have a brother or sister somewhere . . . Surely you can see I have to know. I can't just say, 'Oh my father might be dead — too bad.' . . . Well, can I?'

That was unfair of me, and remembering it now I felt ashamed. After all it can't have been easy for Mum who, even though I knew she'd been happy with Roger all these years, could still, on the rare occasions when my real father's name came into the conversation, look as sad and misty eyed as any heartbroken teenager.

'It's out of the question,' she'd said then. 'Where would you start?'

'I'd start in Perth. That was the last postmark and anyway, I have my friend, Jenny, living there. You remember my friend from college — the one who went on to be a flight attendant and ended up marrying an Aussie? I've put her up before now when she's managed to wangle a cheap trip over. She'll have me for a while, I'm sure.'

The anxious light refused to go from Mum's eyes. 'Perth is hardly the hub of the music business,' she said. 'Anyway he's bound to have changed since the eighties. Definitely will have changed, I should say . . . It'll be like looking for a needle in a haystack.'

'Look, Mum,' I explained as patiently as I could. 'I know it's a long shot. But most of Brad's communications have come from Australia. He spent a lot of time in Perth — that much he told you. We've had postmarks from Sydney, Adelaide, Perth and that Margaret River place, where you said he once told you was a pretty area but he couldn't wait to get away from . . . Surely that's got to be the area for me to try.'

Mum sighed and shook her head. 'Well, you know I can't stop you. In a way I wish I could come with you, but . . . '

'I know — there's Dad, I mean Roger, and honestly I don't expect you to come. I'm a big girl now and besides, it's something I feel I have to do.'

Only now, sitting in my aisle seat with my complimentary white wine and peanuts on the tray in front of me, I didn't feel like a big girl. I felt about five years old and scared. I was missing home, Mum and Andy. But not necessarily in that order.

2

We'd left Heathrow in the late afternoon. I thought that would be excellent, as by the time I'd had the flight meal I'd be tired and ready to sleep. I didn't kid myself I'd sleep like a baby, but thought that at least I'd doze.

Excitement didn't seem to have affected my appetite, but then, not much does. I ate everything on my tray baring the plastic dishes, then worked out how to wind back the film I'd chosen to its beginning. I then spent a good few minutes in securing my headphones so they didn't slip off my head and I could actually hear what was going on. Then, just when I'd done all this, the lady sitting in the window seat in my row wanted to get out.

I smiled politely, stood and flattened myself in the aisle, as the rather large lady squeezed past me. Someone was coming towards me from the other direction. Looking handsomely sulky, in a beautifully cut blue shirt the colour of his eyes, I recognised the guy I was sure I knew but who'd blanked me earlier. Well, I wasn't going to give him a second chance. Avoiding all eye contact, I regained my seat and busied myself in readjusting my headphones.

The film was quite good, but I found concentration difficult. Where, oh where had I seen that guy before? Was it at a party, or an evening out somewhere? More likely to have been at one of the fitness clubs I worked for. Vainly I searched my memory trying to picture him pounding the running machine against a background of fitness equipment. Without even hearing him speak I knew that he had an Australian accent. Now how would I know that if I'd never met him before?

Covertly I watched out of the corner of my eye for Blue Shirt to make his reappearance. He was standing up by the emergency door chatting to one of the air hostesses who was smiling and fluttering her lashes at him — something he was clearly not adverse to. When she'd gone about her duties he continued to linger there doing some kind of strange stretching exercises that involved sticking out his chest with his arms linked behind his back.

I could have instructed him as to the correct way to perform those exercises — after all I am a fitness coach. I gave myself a secret smile, I could see from his powerful shoulders and flat torso that although he may not work out regularly he was a pretty fit specimen. My eyes travelled on up his body until they met his which were twinkling with amusement. Mortified, I hurriedly dropped my gaze back to the video screen and the next time I sneaked a casual glance in his direction, he'd gone.

I watched the film, then wrapped myself in the blanket provided and tried to sleep. Despite the confines of the seats and the drone of the engine I suppose I must have dropped off for a while, because the next thing I knew the captain was talking about landing in Singapore where we had to change flights.

Feeling well and truly jetlagged I followed all the other passengers out of the plane and into the spotlessly clean airport. I found an unostentatious corner and did some arm and leg movements to aid my blood circulation, then wandered around aimlessly for about half an hour, trying to bring some life back into my squashed up body.

My water bottle was empty so I bought more before finding my way back to the gate for the ongoing flight to Perth. My fellow travellers were looking slightly sad and bedraggled now. Our body clocks were telling us this was the middle of the night and we really should be tucked up in bed.

I opened my newspaper again. Then I blinked rapidly, and wished the earth would open up and swallow me.

There in the middle of my paper,

centre fold was a large photo of Blue Shirt. Did I know him? Of course I knew him, along with any other person who took the remotest interest in minor celebrities in the media. Only Nick Packer wasn't a celebrity as such only a fringe worker. He was the current manager and boyfriend of Dee Daniels, the Australian soap opera star who'd just cut a record that had shot right to the top of every hit parade ever invented.

The two of them had done several TV chat show interviews together. My eyes on stalks, I avidly read the blurb which accompanied the scowling image of Nick, hustling an equally grim faced Dee, into a London hotel foyer.

There was rumour of a break up. Although they had been together for the last six months and in spite of the influence that Nick, who handled the sales of a prominent record label, had on her career, it seemed that Dee wanted out of the relationship — both personal and professional.

Goodness. No wonder the poor guy had blanked me. Probably thought I was some kind of desperate wanna-be famous geek or else a journalist in search of a scoop. Surreptitiously I looked round to see if I could spot him. I didn't know whether I was disappointed or relieved when I didn't. Perhaps he wasn't going on to Perth after all. He was more likely to be staying over in a posh hotel in Singapore for a few days and then flying on to Sydney.

I gathered up my belongings and straggled on to the plane, envious at how fresh and bright the flight attendants appeared, before realising that they were of course a different set. My seat allocation was not so good this time — I was in the middle of a row of three. That meant that I would be twice as likely to take a seat belt belonging to somebody else or spill tea in their lap. The window seat passenger was already seated. She was a girl of about my own age who gave me a quick smile then went back to her book.

I arranged my pillow and blanket under my feet from where I hoped I could grab them with a minimum of fuss, installed my water bottle in the seat pouch in front of me and hoped the next six hours would pass comfortably and fast.

By now we all seemed to be settled and the flight attendants were checking the overhead compartments, but the aisle seat next to me still was not taken. Great. I put my book and paper, folded at the centre page with Nick's photo looking straight at me, on the empty seat and decided that once the flight was under way I'd move to the aisle seat to give my fellow passenger and myself more room.

It wasn't to be. About two minutes later a hot and dishevelled looking Nick Packer hurried down the aisle towards my neighbouring seat. Oh no! Rigid with shock I sat paralysed while he picked up my book and paper.

'Yours, I believe?' he said.

'Sorry,' I answered grabbing them fast.

He managed to squash his backpack into the overhead locker and sat himself next to me with his knees jammed up hard against the seat in front.

'Sorry,' he said flashing a white even toothed smile at the pretty stewardess. 'I was making a call, hadn't changed my watch, misjudged the time.'

In the space of a moment I watched her face melt from charming but slightly annoyed to smiling and totally bowled over. I didn't blame her — I was feeling pretty bowled over myself.

Right through the take off I sat there in a silent trance. When he wasn't scowling he was very good looking and had a magnetism about him, that even a girl, who up until very recently had had a serious boyfriend, couldn't ignore.

Once we were at an altitude where things felt fairly steady I risked a sidelong glance at him. He put his seat in a reclining position, fished around on the floor for his pillow and put his hand on my leg. Oh lucky leg. It was only the restraint of the seat belt that stopped me catapulting up to the ceiling.

'Oh, so sorry,' he said turning his blue eyed gaze on me full beam. 'Not much room here is there?'

I squeaked some kind of reply and saw his eyes focus on the newspaper picture still sitting in my lap.

'Ah, I see you know who I am.'

'Um, yes I do, but I didn't earlier. You know when I said 'hello' because I thought I knew you. I mean, I really thought I knew you, you know — intimately . . . ' Oh no, this was going from bad to worse. 'No, I didn't mean intimately as in intimately, of course not. I meant like a next door neighbour or someone who lives in your street. You know, you might not know their name but well, you still say hello to them, if you know what I mean . . . ' My voice trailed off miserably.

Now he would really think I was completely mad. But to my surprise, instead of turning away with 'a likely story' look in his eye, he laughed.

'No worries,' he said again. 'People are always thinking they recognise me but not knowing where from. Well, over the last six months anyway. I used to smile back but it got me into all sorts of trouble so I've perfected a cool glance, which is meant to say 'OK. You know me but I haven't the foggiest who you are, so leave me alone'. I guess I still have some work to do on it.'

'No I'd say you got that about right . . . it wasn't till I saw you in the paper that I realised,' I ventured.

Nick pulled a face. 'You and everyone else. The papers make it sound as though I'm running back home in order to lick my wounds.'

'And are you?' I asked, greatly daring.

He gave a rueful grin. 'Maybe a little. But they're not serious wounds, I can assure you. I always knew the relationship was doomed to fail as soon as Dee hit the jackpot which, it would seem, she has. Instead of just me, she has a team of people looking after her interests now, so it's time for me to take a break and then get back to promoting a very promising rock band I've signed up for a couple of gigs.'

'Oh.' It all sounded very impressive, very glamorous.

'Well — what's your excuse?'

'Sorry?'

'For travelling in this cattle truck to the most remote city in the world.'

'Is it?'

'I think so. Well if it isn't, it certainly feels like it. Perth is miles from anywhere.'

'I'm visiting a friend,' I said cagily.

Nick raised his eyebrows. 'Most people from UK are visiting family. My family live in Western Australia. Mum and Dad are both golf fanatics and they sail a bit. When they retired they bought a place at Joondalup on the edge of a golf course. They're happy as sandboys there.'

'Is this, Joondalup — did you say, near Perth?'

'Yep — about half-an-hour on the Mitchel Freeway, but luckily they've held on to a place in Northbridge, that's right in Perth. I'll spend most of my time there I should think. This is your first trip you say?'

I nodded.

'How does it feel?'

'A bit scary, but Jenny my friend, is meeting me at the airport. She lives near Cottesloe Beach. It's meant to be very nice there.'

'Yeah. Cottesloe Beach is great. Watch out for sharks though!'

'You're joking!' But I could see he wasn't.

'No, it doesn't happen often, but there have been some nasty accidents on the beaches in Western Australia.

'You have to be guided by the Coast Guards and not do anything stupid.'

We chatted a bit more after that, about the city of Perth, places I should be sure to visit. The new rock band he was interested in was based in Perth and he told me he had some venues lined up for them, which included a Wine Fest in Margaret River.

'I've heard of Margaret River,' I said. 'It's meant to be a very pretty area, isn't it? But what's a Wine Fest?'

'A Wine Festival. They hold one every year in November at Cowaramup?'

'Where?' These Australian names were proving difficult to get my head round.

'Cowaramup. I suppose it's a funny name, but I've sort of grown up with it. It's only a tiny place. All the wine boutiques and the bigger wine producers in the Margaret River area — they're famous for their wines, get together for a day of wine tasting and live music. It started in the early nineties and it's proved really popular. It's a good day out and being in the music business myself, I love it. You should try to get there.'

'Yes, perhaps I will.'

The inside of the plane was quite subdued now. The lighting was low and most people were either watching a film or sleeping.

'I think we'd better shut up,' I whispered tipping my seat back and pulling my blanket round my shoulders.

Nick grinned. 'Nighty-night,' he whispered back. 'Sleep well.'

In common, I suspect with most of my fellow travellers, I didn't sleep well, but once the flight crew started to move up and down the aisles with the break-fast trolleys I suddenly felt brighter.

Nick was still asleep. He had indecently long eyelashes for a man, and his cheekbones were a fashion photographer's dream. I couldn't help comparing him to Andy. In a beauty contest Nick would win hands down.

Dear Andy, could I really believe it was all over? Why had I allowed this trip to Australia to separate us mentally as well as physically? But then why hadn't Andy been more reasonable — more understanding? Why had he made the suggestion, gentle though it was, that I might be disappointed? That even if I did find my father, he might be some kind of social drop out, who wouldn't want to know me. How could I forgive him for that?

And any way, why hadn't he contacted me before I left? Surely he knew that half the things I'd said about him being selfish and possessive — I didn't really mean. I sighed, a long sigh of regret that I couldn't turn the clock back and somehow make things right between us again.

'That was a sigh from the heart,' said a voice beside me.

'Oh, you're awake.' I grabbed for the toothbrush kindly supplied by the airline. 'Good, I need to go to the loo.'

Half-an-hour-later, having downed most of the breakfast, which wasn't half as bad as seasoned travellers like Nick pretended, I was feeling bright and excited again. Nick seemed on good form too and was soon entertaining me by telling stories about several celebrities that he'd come into contact with. It did cross my mind a couple of times that he was maybe exaggerating a little and he wasn't quite on such first name terms with them as he led me to believe, but it passed the time pleasantly enough.

He was easy to talk to too and a good listener. Before I knew it I had confided in him about my real reason for coming to Perth. I could see he was intrigued, and in the telling of it the romance of the situation hit me afresh.

'I suppose you think I'm mad even to attempt this,' I said.

'No. Not so long as you're realistic about your chances. But the music business is a fairly small world and hey, you already have access to it.'

'You mean you'll help me?'

'Well, sure. I'll put out a few feelers. You'll have to get that photo copied. That's the problem really, the only photo being over twenty years old. People change a lot in twenty years.'

'I thought musicians always have long hair and wear flamboyant clothes?'

'Not if they've gone bald and decided

to change their image.'

I bowed to his superior knowledge. 'Perhaps we can ask around in Perth. The Arts Council, places like that?'

'I'll dig around in my neck of the woods and try my contacts. But,' he shook his head slightly. 'Brad Williams? It just doesn't ring a bell.'

We exchanged mobile phone numbers and he promised to call me if he found anything out. The remainder of the journey seemed to pass in no time with us chatting away as though we'd known each other forever.

It was at the baggage collection that we went our separate ways. I had no false illusions that we'd stay in touch even though he'd hinted as much, but he helped me organise my backpack and luggage, gave me a brief hug and wished me well. Then, with only a feeling of slight regret, I was on my way through customs and out into Perth air terminal where Jenny was waiting to greet me.

3

After the hustle and bustle of Heathrow and the shiny clean elegance of Singapore, Perth Airport seemed very quiet and laid back. Blinking a little at the bright light outside I pushed my trolley through customs. Just a little anxiously, I scanned the collection of friends and relatives waiting to greet loved ones.

'Caro, over here!'

Suddenly I spotted a fair head attached to a small round body which was agitatedly jumping up and down. I felt a beam split my face. It was Jenny.

Squeaking with excitement she hugged and kissed me. 'Did you have a good flight? I love your top. How's your mum? I bet you're hungry. Let me take your bag. Crikey, it weighs a ton. You'll never guess who I've just seen!'

Oh yes, it was Jenny, all right!

'I bet I will,' I said, answering her last statement first. 'What's more he was sitting right next to me on the flight. Well, since Singapore anyway. Wow, it's hot out here. Lovely.'

'You sat next to Nick Packer — I don't believe it! Of all the luck! What was he like? I've heard he's a bit of a heartbreaker. What did he say? Is it true he's broken up with Dee?'

Laughing I struggled with my bags. 'Half a minute. I've only just about landed. Give me a chance to get over my jet lag. First things first. Where's your car? All will be revealed later.'

'Sorry,' said Jenny not looking in the least crestfallen. 'You don't look very jetlagged. You look positively glowing. Still you always have looked impossibly healthy — it's all that fitness training I expect.'

Yep, that must be it. It couldn't possibly have anything to do with a certain Nick Packer who'd given me a hug before he went on his way and promised to ring me the very next day.

The rest of that day passed in a blur. The bright sunlight took a bit of getting used to but wow, it felt great to feel the warmth on my bare arms and to see the high endlessly blue sky above me.

Jenny's house turned out to be a low one storey building. It was what they termed a new build, very spacious with fly screen doors, blinds at every window and air conditioning.

In the evening, when Paul, Jenny's husband, arrived home we shared a bottle of wine sitting out under their patio roof, which had been built to give added shade to both the interior and exterior.

'This is the life,' I said pulling a sweater round my shoulders because the sun had suddenly disappeared and a chill had arrived as though from nowhere.

'It's still nippy in the evenings this time of year. Are you cold? Shall we go in?' Paul was all attention.

I shook my head. 'Not on your life. It's . . .' I looked at my watch, 'seven-thirty, it's November and I'm outside drinking wine. If I were at home I'd be sitting on the tube trying to avoid other people's coughs and sneezes, looking forward to an evening indoors with the television and a mug of hot chocolate . . . Please don't make me go in yet.'

We sat in silence for a while. I was marvelling at the hibiscus and jasmine flowering at the side of the patio. The flowers looked to be twice the size of those at home, yet they were growing out of what looked like sand, and their scent was just heavenly. I breathed in deeply, savouring the moment, but my peace was shattered by the sound of my mobile phone.

It was Mum. It was lovely to hear her voice. I assured her I was all right and promised to e-mail her and tell her all about my adventures so far. 'Oh and make sure you contact Andy,' Mum finished. 'He's been driving me mad because he didn't have your new mobile number and hasn't heard from you.'

'Really,' I said in a frozen voice. 'OK then I suppose I'd better e-mail him, tell him I've arrived safely, although I'm surprised he cares.'

'Of course he cares,' said Mum. 'You must e-mail him, Caro, you owe him that at least.'

We said our goodbyes and I tucked my phone back in my bag with a sigh.

'Problems?' asked Jenny. 'Sounds like boyfriend trouble.'

'You could say that.'

'Andy — he's the one you thought could be serious?'

I gave a laugh that was more of a snort. 'Yeah he can be serious all right. When I told him I was coming here to search for my real father, he got really serious. Doom and gloom personified. Seems to think I don't stand an earthly chance of finding him and even if I do, he'll be some kind of fiend who will latch on to me and take all my money and then throw me out. In short I will be bitterly disappointed and it will ruin the rest of my life. Therefore I should let sleeping dogs lie.'

Jenny didn't say anything for a long time. Paul went inside for more biscuits and cheese and I stared at my glass trying to hate Andy for being wrong on every count.

'You've obviously considered the possibility that Andy could be right?' Jenny asked lightly.

'He won't be right,' I said with a conviction that I was not entirely feeling. 'The man, my father, has sent me something every birthday for as long as I can remember. Every single year! He's never, ever missed. Doesn't that say something?'

The night was very dark, the stars extraordinarily bright. I turned the glass in my hand then watched as Jenny refilled it.

'Yes, it says that he's a romantic. It says that he doesn't want you to forget that he's out there somewhere. But face it, Caro, he's never written to ask how you feel about him leaving you. He's never given you a return address so you could say 'help Dad, I could do with some support', has he?'

This was so near to what Andy had pointed out to me the last time we spoke that I practically burst into tears. I tried to pull myself together and be rational.

'OK I know what you're saying. You don't want me to be disappointed. It's all right, Jenny, believe me, I know what I'm doing. I'm going into it with my eyes open. It's just that if I don't do this now, I feel I may never get the opportunity again. I've just got to try. I've just got to.'

I suppose I must have been more tired than I wanted to admit because to my horror my words ended on a sob. Jenny's small hand shot across the table and covered mine. 'I understand,' she said. 'I just wanted to be sure you'd considered what the outcome could be.'

'I've done nothing but consider it,' I wobbled. 'But I'm still going for it.'

We looked at each other squarely across the table.

'That's great,' she said. 'But right now, well as soon as you've finished your wine, you're going to bed. You've got lots of sleep to catch up on.'

Despite falling asleep directly I snapped the light out, I found myself troubled by strange dreams involving losing my luggage and not being able to find a taxi or Andy. However, the next morning I was soon able to put them behind me and concentrate on the here and now. Jenny suggested a fairly easy day. She produced a map of Perth and offered to show me round.

This was a plan I was more than happy to fall in with because although I wanted to get on and start tracing my dad I had to confess I had little idea of where to start. But it could wait for a day while I got myself acclimatised and became familiar with the general layout of the area.

Jenny explained that she usually used the train to travel to and from Perth for quick shopping expeditions. 'Parking can be difficult and train travel is cheap and easy.'

It was. The station at Cottesloe was only five minutes walk away from Jenny's house in one direction — the beach only five minutes in the other. 'We're really lucky,' she said. 'I can't ever imagine wanting to live anywhere else.' On this wonderful morning, I could well believe it.

Cottesloe station turned out to consist of just a couple of platforms and tracks — you would never believe you were so close to a major city, but Perth Railway Station when we arrived there about twenty minutes later, was a much larger affair. Well, not large by London standards, and it still put me in mind of a quieter gentler time gone by, but it was busy and an expansion seemed to be taking place to the side of it so Perth looked to be a prosperous expanding city.

'Northbridge, where you said Nick Packer hangs out, is to the north of the station,' explained Jenny. 'But we're

41

going this way, south towards the centre and the shops and if we keep going a couple of blocks we reach The Swan River, which is really lovely.'

★   ★   ★

That first morning in Perth, the impressions I picked up were of a clean, new city busy with lots of coffee-carrying business people in sharp light suits nipping between high buildings. I soon worked out that the main roads were planned on a grid system, which made it almost impossible to get lost. But I still clung on to my map and spent a lot of time turning it upside down because somehow the sun was never where I expected it to be.

'Of course it is,' said Jenny when I complained to her that I was finding it confusing and couldn't get my bearings. 'It's in the sky. You poor thing, it's because you haven't seen it for so long, you've forgotten what it looks like — you definitely needed this holiday.'

'It's not that. It's in a different direction. It's to do with hemispheres,' I defended myself.

'Come on, put the geography lesson on hold, I want to show you this shop, the fashions are quite advanced here, not quite like London — but we're getting there.'

Well, it's always fascinating to look at unfamiliar shops and as we were going into summer here, the clothes were deliciously light and floaty, and at tempting prices. My wardrobe was mostly made up of last year's T-shirts, jeans and sports pants, perhaps I should look out for a pretty strappy dress just in case I was invited out to dinner by . . .

'What are you looking so goo-eyed about?' asked Jenny.

'Nothing,' I answered. 'Nothing at all.'

After we'd had a cup of coffee, a flat white, they called it here, Jenny wanted to show me the internet café-come-travel agents where she worked although not today because she'd taken time off to be with me.

The premises were situated just off the main shopping precinct and were smart and clean. They ran a good system. For a nominal amount you could buy a cup of coffee and use the internet for thirty minutes.

I quickly rattled off an e-mail to Mum giving a brief summary of my trip so far, then *cc'd* it to several friends including Andy.

For some reason I balked at the idea of sending him a personal message just at the moment. Particularly since, despite his reported anxiety as to my welfare, he hadn't left an e-mail for me, I noticed.

After that we made our way towards the Swan River and looked around the ferry terminal where you could take trips to Freemantle or Rottnest Island. The water was clear and sparkling and we decided to take a leisurely stroll along the riverside.

The peace was only interrupted now

and then by a jogger or cyclist, so we were able to fill each other in with more details of how our lives had shaped up since we'd last been together. Jenny admitted that she still suffered from home sickness but that she wouldn't change her life with Paul for anything.

'It's the people I've left behind though. If only Perth were say, where Spain is relative to England, I'd be so happy.'

'So would everyone else. This wouldn't be as it is though; it would be totally spoiled, completely overrun by tourists. You have to face it, you can't have everything. The only really idyllic places left are all at the back of beyond.'

Jenny tucked her arm in mine in order to steer me out of the way of a passing cyclist whose special path we were sharing. 'You're right,' she said.

On the walk back we stopped for lunch at a small café right on the waterfront. We sat outside of course, where we could hear and see the gently lapping water. I ate my salad and chips with the relish that only comes when eating in the fresh air.

Suddenly I stopped chewing, eyes transfixed to the blue water about fifteen feet out. No, it couldn't be!

'You won't believe this,' I squeaked after nearly choking on a mouthful of lettuce. 'I thought I saw a dolphin.'

'Yep, that would be possible.'

'A dolphin really? Why didn't you tell me?'

'Tell you what?'

'To look for dolphins, of course. I mean right here so close to the shoreline?' My phoned started trilling in my bag. Still in a state of shock, I leapt to my feet and answered.

'Hello, this is Nick.'

'Nick? Oh — Nick. You'll never guess what Nick. I've just seen a dolphin right here. I'm just eating my lunch with Jenny and this dolphin — well, it just swam by.'

'Really? Well, that was cool. How about dinner tonight?'

'Oh well, yes. That sounds good.'

What did I mean? It sounded fantastic.

'Good.'

'Lovely,' I sat down again, all thoughts of dolphins chased from my brain. Maybe I could just nip back and buy the strappy little dress I'd seen earlier.

'Well?' Nick was still on the phone.

'Well what?'

An exasperated sigh sounded in my ear. 'I can tell I'm no competition for a dolphin, but I've been thinking about you a lot and I'd really like to see you again. But I need to know where you're staying so I can pick you up.'

I sat down fairly quickly. 'I can get the train. I could meet you at Perth station.'

'That sounds cool.'

Trying to ignore Jenny frantically waving at me to get him to pick me up from home, I arranged a time with Nick — seven-thirty, which sounded extremely early to me but which I later found was about the norm for Perth, then rang off.

Nonchalantly I picked up my fork. 'Well?'

My cheeks were burning. 'Don't say 'well?' like that. It's only dinner.'

'Hmm!'

★   ★   ★

The strappy dress fitted perfectly but the effect was spoilt a little because I had to wear my military style jacket over the top in order to hide the goose bumps that arrived without fail as the sun went down. I had to remind myself that although daytime temperatures were hotter than our summer, it was still only spring in Perth.

Nick met me just outside the station. At the mere sight of him my stomach started fluttering. He really was the ultimate in cool. He was dressed very casually in lightweight trousers and a white shirt with a navy sweater slung across his shoulders.

'Hi,' he said. 'You look gorgeous.'

'Thanks,' I mumbled unused to

receiving compliments.

'Mmm. You smell gorgeous too.' He draped an arm round my shoulders and gave me a squeeze.

Well, what's a girl to do? You've got to smile haven't you? You've got to be polite. Anyway, dull old Andy had never told me I smelled gorgeous and Andy was on the other side of the world.

We walked to an area, which was full of restaurants.

'How d'you feel about fish?'

'Love it. Well, as long as it's not dolphin.'

'Dolphins are mammals.'

'I know that, of course I know that.'

The service in the fish restaurant was laid back but very friendly. In no time we were sitting at a well positioned table attended by a starry eyed waitress who presented us with a complimentary bottle of wine. Fame and being recognised obviously has its compensations.

Tucked into a corner at the back was a guy with a guitar strapped to his back and not long after we were seated he started to play a few well known ballads. The evening was beginning to take on a feeling of intimacy.

After the starter of avocado with some gigantic prawns, I went on to have barramundi, the most delicious fish I've ever eaten. It was cooked simply yet beautifully with just a hint of lemons and herbs.

'Mmm, this is lovely.'

'Thought you'd like it.' He was so confident. Briefly I wondered what he would have said had I put down my knife and fork and declared it was inedible. But that was plain stupid, I pushed the thought away.

'Have you thought about where to start looking for your dad?'

'Not really. The usual official channels I suppose. Find out about deaths in the area over the past, say, fifteen months. Check the electoral roll. That sort of thing I suppose. Why, have you any suggestions?'

'I've already put out a few feelers

amongst my music buddies. No luck, I'm afraid. No-one's heard of a Bradley Williams and of course when I tell them his approximate age it doesn't help because so many youngsters start off in music, full of good intentions in their twenties but have opted out completely by the time their mid thirties come along. You could be looking for a successful mid forty-year-old business-man, not an ageing hippy.'

For some reason, that hurt. 'I never said he was an ageing hippy . . . I do know he's travelled around a lot, but his most usual postmark was Perth, which would fit with the idea of touring, wouldn't it? And Mum always felt he'd stick to music.'

Nick shrugged. 'Well, so long as you realise it's not going to be easy.'

This wasn't what I wanted to hear. First Jenny, now Nick warning me I may not succeed and I'd only been here a day.

My phone chose that moment to trill. 'Oh sorry. I meant to turn it off.' I groped in my bag. It was Andy. For a moment I was tempted not to answer. Then I thought of his serious face, thought of the tender look he sometimes had in his eyes when he was unaware I was watching him and suddenly I knew that Andy's was the voice I wanted to hear more than anything else in the world.

4

Hi,' Andy's voice came cold and stilted down the line. How I wished I were taking this call with no audience. 'Hi,' I answered equally ill at ease.

'Thanks for the e-mail.'

'Oh, you got it.'

'Yes.'

This was insane. We were talking like two polite strangers. Then there was a loud burst of laughter from the neighbouring table and the guitarist finished his piece to a round of applause. The sound of it must have travelled over the phone.

'Where are you?'

'I'm having dinner with a friend.'

There was a long pause, which for some reason I didn't want to be the first to break.

'Oh, right. I'd better go then.' His voice was even chillier.

'No, it's all right . . . It's — it's um — business. Nick's just using his contacts to help me trace my dad.'

Silence.

'You know. I told you in my e-mail.'

'Nick as in Nick Packer?' His voice was full of suspicion.

'That's right. He's being very helpful as it happens.'

'Well, clearly, you're very busy. I'd better go.'

'E-mail me, won't you?' I said miserably.

'As it happens, I'm busy too. But yes, all right and Caro . . . '

'Yes?'

'Please take care.'

'Sorry,' I said as I clicked off. 'I don't usually take calls when I'm at a restaurant.'

'No worries.' But Nick did look a bit miffed. 'Who was it?' he said eventually. 'Your mum?'

'No, not my mum. Just a friend.'

'A concerned friend?'

'Well, yes. He ought to be concerned,

but perhaps he isn't.'

'Oh dear,' said Nick looking brighter and much more interested. 'The *Man You Left Behind,* eh?'

I was feeling angry now. How dare Andy ring me up, then just ring off without even saying he missed me or wishing me luck or anything any other remotely human person would do?

'Yeah, well. That was his choice,' I said shortly.

'Not interested in your family tree then?'

'I suppose not. Anyway he had work commitments.'

'Work commitments,' repeated Nick. 'What's he like then? What's he do?'

What was he like? 'He's big,' I said eventually. 'Well over six foot. He's nice. Well, not all the time. Sometimes he's infuriating.' I was remembering our last face to face conversation. When I wanted him to beg me not to go — say he couldn't live without me. To declare his love for me. Ha! Fat chance. Instead he'd warned me about disappointment and talked about work commitments! 'And he's a plumber.'

'A plumber?' The derision in Nick's voice was obvious. 'A plumber?' he said again.

'Spare me the jokes about U bends,' I said jumping to Andy's defence. 'He happens to be a very good plumber, he's just picked up a wonderful contract for a new property development.'

'Sounds very exciting. I bet he's flushed with success.' I decided to let that one go and watched as the waitress came and removed our plates.

Nick swilled his wine around in his glass. 'It's a long way to come if you leave your heart behind you,' he said.

I smiled. 'That sounds like the opening line of a song. Country and Western I would guess. But in answer to your thinly veiled question. No, I haven't left my heart in London. Andy and I — we needed a break and we had no real commitment.'

'No, doesn't sound like it. After all why would anyone who cared, let you try to do this mammoth task you've set yourself all alone?'

'Yes, why would they?'

I threw myself whole heartedly into the evening after that. Some other diners who knew Nick came in and we joined them at their table. They seemed to be a friendly crowd. Perhaps a shade more glossy than my friends at home and maybe they laughed a little louder and surreptitiously glanced over one another's shoulders in case someone more interesting should appear, but I suppose living in the world of the nearly famous did that to you.

They hovered round Nick as though just by being near him a little of his sparkle would rub off. Then I chided myself for being cynical and determined instead, to join in the fun. Because, it was fun.

Nick's friends were all very outspoken and amusing and soon practically lining up to ask me questions about the London scene, imagining no doubt, that because I worked and lived in

London, I must spend my life bumping into celebrities.

At the end of quite a long evening, Paddy, one of Nick's friends, offered to drive me home. Nick sat in the back with me and draped a casual arm round my shoulders. Even though by this time I could barely keep my eyes open and was smothering yawns every thirty seconds or so, I felt the tingle of attraction slithering from his fingers where they touched my bare arm, all the way down to my toes.

But all too soon we reached Jenny's house.

Nick pulled me closer. I stopped breathing. 'See you soon, babe,' he said easily, kissing me casually on the cheek. 'I'll call you.'

★ ★ ★

I spent the next morning on Jenny's computer catching up with e-mails again and sending fresh ones enquiring after any possible trace of Brad

Williams. I phoned various contacts that Nick had given me, explaining who I was and that Bradley Williams was a singer songwriter, but played piano and guitar. I explained how old he was; that he'd spent time in England; gave brief descriptions and offered to send copies of the twenty-two-year-old much treasured photo. All to no avail.

As my mother had indicated, Perth was not the hub of Australia's music industry. But that was one of the reasons I'd hoped it might be easier to trace him there. It somehow seemed likely to me that since he spent a lot of his time in Perth, surely he would hang out with his cronies — and they were bound to be musical, weren't they? So, logic told me, if I had an 'in' to the small musical world in Perth then surely I would find him.

So it was in a more subdued mood that I met up with Nick in the afternoon. I thought I'd got used to the stares that accompanied him wherever he went, but today, in daylight, I found it began to irritate. He so obviously loved it.

'G'day. How're you doing?' he kept saying every time someone gave him a second glance. Some of his fans looked at me too which I found rather disconcerting, especially since I'd not given too much thought as to what I was wearing and it really was much too hot a day for more than a lick of make up.

The recording studio we were going to was in Northbridge again, and I had to admit that the district we were wandering into was rather unattractive, unlike the lovely shopping precinct or the area where we'd eaten the evening before. However, Nick insisted that there would be lots of roadsters there — people who knew people.

There were, but none of them it seemed, had ever heard of Brad Williams. They were friendly enough and I watched fascinated through smoky glass as a girl and guy, both with sun-bleached jaggedly fashioned hair and jeans, cut a 'demo' disc.

Nick kept shaking his head and looking critical, but when they'd finished offered to buy them a drink in the next door bar.

The girl whose name was Jo, was very sweet and seemed too naïve to be in the rock business. Her boyfriend, I assumed it was her boyfriend, and Nick were talking heavy rock bands and gigs and what was the line up at the Margaret River Fest, so running out of small talk, I fumbled in my bag for my photo of my dad.

'This is why I'm in Perth really,' I explained to Jo. 'I'm looking for my dad.'

Jo looked surprised. 'Oh, I thought Nick brought you over from UK? Thought you were his new girlfriend?'

I was later to discover that every statement Jo made came out like a question. It was a fairly common Australian trait but never quite so obvious as on Jo.

'No, I'm not his girlfriend,' I said

quickly fighting down a blush. 'We're just good mates.'

Something in Jo's expression told me she didn't believe me but then she caught sight of the photo. 'Hang on. How old did you say this guy would be now?'

My heart started hammering against my ribs. 'Mid to late forties . . . Why? D'you think you recognise him?'

But Jo pushed the photo back into my hand. 'Nah. Can't be. Just something about the nose? The guy I was thinking about was a friend of my dad's — up in Adelaide? Never knew his other name. Got a daughter in England that's all?'

'Well, does it look like him?' I knew already the answer to that. I was clutching at straws.

Jo looked at me with sympathy in her eyes. 'No sorry, couldn't really say — could be his nose . . . I think it was the daughter, father thing. Sort of threw me? But no — I don't think so.'

Then she turned away to listen to

what her boyfriend and Nick were discussing so avidly and the next moment she was laughing. I didn't feel like joining in. Moodily I stared at my flat white and wondered what on earth I was doing sitting in this dingy, smoky bar listening to talk I didn't understand about jazz, rock, hip-hop, blues and audio equipment.

Then, just as I was feeling at my most alone, Nick's hand with its long lean fingers came to rest on top of mine. I looked up at him and he smiled deep into my eyes and my insides melted. 'What's the worry?' he asked. 'What's with the frown? Not bored are you?'

'Of course not,' I lied. 'Jet lag catching up I expect.'

'You're up for it then?'

'Up for what?' I asked suspiciously.

'The Wine Fest. Haven't you been listening?'

This was moving a little fast. 'Um, I don't know.'

'If you want to trace your father and Margaret River was somewhere he spoke about and he mailed you from there, I think you should, don't you?'

Immediately I felt better. 'Well, perhaps.'

'No 'perhaps' about it. We can kill two birds with one stone. Have a great time there. Chill out with the music and the wine. I might get me a few deals. You might find your dad. Got to be good.'

Put like that, Nick was right. It had to be good. Hadn't it?

★ ★ ★

Jenny wasn't so keen on the idea. 'Look it's one thing meeting up with him for dinner. But to go away with him for what amounts to the weekend . . . Well, I just don't think you know him well enough that's all.'

'You're beginning to sound like my mother.'

'Well, don't get carried away with this Nick Packer. He has quite a reputation you know, and it's not all good. He's had loads of girlfriends. He's a lady killer. A rat.'

'Any moment now and you'll say he's a cad and a bounder.'

'Undoubtedly he is.'

'Bit of a change of heart. I seem to remember you being thrilled to bits when you knew I'd been sitting next to him on the plane.'

Jenny's expression was uncharacteristically serious. 'One thing sitting on a plane, quite another going on a jolly.'

'Oh, come on, Jen. He's just a friend. We're not sharing a room or anything. I'm not stupid . . . How else would I get another chance like this? I'm going to Margaret River which I have reason to believe is somewhere my father stayed or lived, I have transport there, an introduction to the music makers in that neck of the woods, and there's this wine festival on. What could be more perfect?'

In the end Jenny had to agree that it was too good an opportunity to pass by. 'Just be careful,' she said. 'Nick Packer comes from a wealthy family and he's used to getting exactly what he wants. Don't let yourself be talked into anything you might regret.'

I opened my mouth to ask 'such as?' Then closed it again because of course I knew perfectly well.

There were another two days before I was due to go to the Wine Fest with Nick. Nick had already told me that he would probably be spending those days catching up with his family in Joondalup. I was quite relieved it would give me time to sort out something that was on my mind.

As soon as I explained to Jenny that I really needed some sort of part time work to boost my meagre savings she contacted a friend who owned a breakfast bar in the business area of Perth.

'Anna's always looking for casual staff for the morning shift,' she said. 'It's quite relaxed you just take the customers orders and serve them. You can't go wrong.'

I trained it into Perth next day along

with Jenny, who introduced me to Anna, then left me to have a practice run while she went off to work. The waitressing uniform consisted of a white T-shirt, black trousers and a white headband with a net attached to keep your hair tidy. I was very glad Nick wouldn't be in the business area of Perth between seven and ten in the morning. The head gear was far from attractive.

I was introduced to the other workers who seemed a friendly bunch, and familiarised myself with the selection of mueslis, fruits and yoghurts on the display counter. I knew what a flat white was by now and I hastily scanned the menu card for any other terminology that might throw me, but thankfully it all seemed pretty self-explanatory.

'OK, I'm going to throw you in the deep end. The guy with the silver cropped hair sitting outside reading the paper — he's one of our regulars. He'll order a flat white, wholemeal toast and jam. Try him.'

Feeling ridiculously nervous I approached the table Anna had pointed out.

'Good morning. What can I get you?'

The guy looked up and gave me a blue, twinkly-eyed smile. ' 'Morning,' he said. 'I'll have a flat white and two slices of wholemeal toast please.'

'Jam to go with that?'

'You must have read my mind.'

This was easy. My next order was from a couple who had eyes only for each other. Love's young dream as my mother would say. They wanted a black coffee and a mineral water and then they shared a fresh fruit salad and yoghurt.

After that it suddenly got busy and, before I knew it, I was dodging between tables, putting in orders, fetching extra sugars or paper napkins and mopping up spilled milk without noticing the time.

'Thanks Caro — you're a star,' said Anna when things had calmed down again. 'That was great for a first time. Now I know you can't do Friday or the weekend, but I'll expect you tomorrow and then on Monday.'

I felt a glow of achievement. 'OK,' I said. 'I'm looking forward to it.' And I found I was.

For a moment I was tempted to ring Nick and tell him about my waitressing debut, but somehow I didn't think it would go down well. It wasn't that I thought he would disapprove exactly, it was just — well, I just didn't want to — that was all.

5

I thought that Nick and I would have company on our drive to Margaret River, but when at midmorning the next day he came and collected me, he was alone with his car.

Unfortunately, Jenny was already at work. I'm sure she would have approved of the way he helped me with my bags and checked that I had a jacket because this was further south and therefore colder, and she surely would have approved of his car, which was low and red, and purred like a contented animal while I settled myself in.

'We'll meet Paddy, Jo and the others down there. They've got equipment and stuff to organise.' He looked at me critically for a moment. 'We'll have to get you a hat, you'll need one in the daytime. The forecast's good so I hope we can travel down the coast a bit. It's a surfer's paradise.'

Suddenly I felt really happy. Excited, pleased to be alive and just so happy.

'What are you grinning at?'

'I don't know,' I lied. 'The weather probably.'

Being with you, I thought. Sitting in this car, next to this good looking guy, listening to a CD of I knew not what and anticipating a good few days ahead, whether I found my father or not.

That was it. Be more laid back. Enjoy the moment.

Nick kept up a steady stream of witty conversation as we sped along towards our first stop of Mandurah. The sparkling water was lined with spanking new looking boats. We walked along the pretty quayside hand in hand, grabbed ourselves a coffee and bought some bottled water on the jetty, then we climbed back in the car and headed for Pelican Beach where there was nothing much except for large expanses of sand and sea and, oh yes, pelicans.

Nick produced a blanket from the

boot and a cool bag, which contained some delicious looking sandwiches he'd picked up in Perth and some apples and cheese. Even Nick couldn't keep up a steady conversation whilst we ate, although he did still manage a few comments.

For a while we sat watching the ungainly pelicans take flight and come in again to land. They were much bigger than I thought and I was quite glad when we'd finished eating our sandwiches and they lost interest in us.

With a sigh Nick stretched out on the blanket and shut his eyes. Peace at last. I continued to sit up hugging my knees.

'What're you thinking about?' I turned my head to find Nick studying me through lazy, half closed eyes.

'I don't know . . . Just how lucky I am I suppose . . . Seriously Nick, really I am very grateful.'

The peaceful spell was broken and I cleared up the picnic things resolving that I would be paying for the next meal, or drink — because there was no way I wanted to feel obligated to Nick Packer who was too damn attractive for his own good.

Our next stop was Bumbury, which was positioned on a peninsula and surrounded by the waters of the Indian Ocean. In the brochure it was described as a cosmopolitan city, full of life, but to a London girl like me, it felt like my idea of a quiet 1930s seaside town.

There were the remains of war fortifications on the front and lots of Norfolk Pines which, Nick informed me, had been planted in days gone by, so that if ever a ship pulled in, there would be wood available for a replacement mast.

We took a brief walk along the beautiful and deserted beach. It felt as though we were the only two people in the world. A wide expanse of white sand and turquoise sea only broken by occasional volcanic rock gullies, stretched for miles and miles. The weather was still warm but very windy. By the time we returned to the car my legs and face felt as though they'd been sand blasted and my hair straightened into a thick bush by the bracing walk along the dunes.

I said as much to Nick as he sat watching while I tried to repair the damage.

'It's not a perm then? It actually comes out of your head like that?'

'Pardon me?'

'Well, it just sort of cork screws.'

'Thanks for that,' I said, not knowing whether to be amused or angry. He gave a laugh. 'Sorry. Didn't mean to upset you, and you are very beautiful. But curls just aren't cool. Curls are fun. Cute and girlie.'

'Is that so?'

'Believe me it's so. What you need is a lighter look. Take a bit of the frizz out — then a shiner and straightener . . . You could look so fabulous.'

What was he — a hairdresser now?

'As opposed to frightful you mean?'

Nick grinned. 'Not frightful. You wouldn't be sitting here with me if you looked frightful . . . But not as drop dead gorgeous as you could be either.'

Hold on, was that an insult or a compliment? I thought for a moment and decided to let it go.

'So, wait a minute. You think you could make me drop dead gorgeous?'

'You'd better believe it.'

How shallow, I thought. Then I looked in the driving mirror at my wild hair and shiny face. Not drop dead gorgeous at all.

Nick passed the map to me, not so that I could direct him, he could drive to Margaret River blind folded he assured me, though I was glad he didn't actually put it to the test, but just so I could see where we were heading.

'I was thinking of going over to Dunsborough then along the coast road through Grace Town. There are some stunning views on the west coast, but I think when we reach Busselton maybe we'll take the Busselton Highway all the way through Cowaramup to Margaret River. It'll be quicker. We can do the scenic route on the way back. What d'you think?'

I studied the map and agreed.

Busselton Highway proved to be a lush leafy sweep of roadway lined with fields and vineyards and so unlike any highway I'd ever come across before that I was speechless.

'This is beautiful,' I said. 'What are those tall pink gladiola flowers?'

Nick just shrugged. 'I dunno,' he said. 'The woods are full of them. They grow wild.'

I stopped asking questions after that, just sat back and enjoyed the view until we reached Margaret River which proved to be another, to me, small town full of charm and character.

The hotel when we found it, with its wooden porches and air of shabby gentility, again seemed to belong in an old film and not in this millennium at all.

'We'll eat at eight,' said Nick. 'There's a super fish place in the main street but it doesn't have a licence so

I'll take the wine. I'll give you a knock at quarter to.'

'Right,' I said. 'I'll be ready.'

★ ★ ★

The evening was much cooler. We walked through the quiet unlit streets to the 'fish place'. At first glance, it didn't look like much, but I couldn't have been more wrong. Once again, as soon as we were over the threshold, Nick received a lot of attention. He was greeted with cries of delight and spent a long time exchanging news, about people I'd never heard of, along with the owner. I was introduced as a mate looking for her dad — Brad — Bradley Williams.

I waited with anticipation.

'Never heard of him.'

Oh well, what had I expected? Never mind I was here now and I might as well make the best of it. I contemplated the list of appetising food in front of me and sniffed appreciatively at the mouth watering smells coming from the kitchen. I would not let myself be dispirited; after all, I had hardly started looking for my dad yet. I turned my full attention to the menu. Somehow I didn't fancy kangaroo or ostrich, but wanted to try something new so I ordered Dhu fish.

The restaurant started to fill and about fifty per cent of the customers appeared to be long lost buddies of Nick's. I began to feel just a little bit out of it. They included me, of course they did, and I can't say Nick ignored me exactly, but all the same I hadn't bargained on sharing him with quite so many admirers.

I'd finished my meal now and had to admit that the ingredients were perfect and it was cooked to perfection. With a murmured excuse Nick had wandered off to the back of the room where I could just make him out as he bent to listen to a blonde with a very low neckline.

I smiled to myself; it made a change

to see Nick actually listening instead of talking.

I helped myself to another glass of wine. A girl dressed all in black but for a red pashmina draped over her shoulders, sat herself down in Nick's seat.

'Nick tells me you're coming tomorrow? To the Wine Fest,' she added by way of explanation. 'That's great. You'll have a terrific time. Remember to get yourself a hat. There are a few gazebos around but it's held in a couple of fields so there's not a lot of shelter from the sun.

There was something about her I liked. Something theatrical, maybe slightly dramatic; what with the black hair and clothes, the white face and the slash of red lips to match her pashmina.

I asked her if she was in the music business. Expecting her to tell me she was a singer.

'No, not me. I'm in the wine business. I'm manning one of the stands. I'll be pouring the samples and trying to make sure that if they buy anything it will be from us.'

'And who's us?' I asked. 'So I'll know who to look for.'

'Oh there's so many there you'll forget. Bradford Wines. We're not well known — just a family business really.'

'A Wine Boutique,' I said coining a phrase I'd heard Nick use.

'Yeah I suppose so. We were established in the late sixties and picked up on the new trend of blending the wines so we always managed a reasonable year. The Australian wine trade is very young though — there's tremendous room for growth.'

'It's a very beautiful area,' I said trying to please but also meaning it. 'It's much more lush here than at Perth, and the wild flowers are amazing. I saw a farmer hacking away at a huge clump of arum lilies — I couldn't believe my eyes — they were growing wild!'

Natasha, because I'd discovered that was her name, laughed. 'Yes, it's a great place to live, especially now while it's buzzing. But it can be very quiet, the night life's not up to much.'

Just then Nick sauntered back and after a few words about looking out for her stand the next day, she said she had to get an early night in because tomorrow would be tough, and left with a crowd of about six others.

'She was nice,' I commented to Nick.

'Yeah. Comes from one of the most successful wine families in the area.'

'Oh, she said theirs was a small family business?'

'Small, maybe. Exclusive — certainly.'

'I've never heard of Bradford Wines in England.'

Nick gave a short laugh. 'No, you wouldn't have. They don't make enough to export. It's expensive stuff — comparable to the best French wines. They say that Margaret River make the greatest collection of Chardonnays. The Wine Boutiques have problems providing for the home market so they don't really need to advertise, but the Wine Fest is something they have to support because they're just as important to the area as the big concerns.'

Nick gave his full attention to me after that. Making sure my glass was full, looking deep into my eyes, assuring me that tomorrow he would leave no stone unturned in trying to find my dad. I listened and I believed him.

When we left the restaurant and the late evening air hit me I realised I'd probably had one glass of wine too many. I was still able to walk straight, but had to think very carefully about every word before I said it, just in case it slurred. Jenny would not have approved.

We walked back to the hotel and it seemed natural that I should enjoy the sensation of Nick's arm around my shoulders.

'Thanks for a lovely evening, Nick,' I said when we reached my door.

'No, thank you,' replied Nick ever the gentleman. 'We didn't have coffee. Shall

I come in for a cup?'

The light catching his face, seeking out the planes and the shadows, made him look like a young Greek god. I was very tempted, but I thought of Jenny, and regretfully shook my head. 'Not a good idea,' I said.

Nick leaned forward and kissed me. Perhaps it was because he took me by surprise but instead of pushing him away as I should have done, I found myself responding and wishing the moment could last forever. Wishing that I wasn't here to find my dad; that Andy wasn't still in London waiting for my return and that I only had myself to please. Myself and Nick.

'You sure about that?' asked Nick in a whisper, still holding me close.

I'd never been so unsure about anything in my life. But I was a long way from home, and I was here for a reason.

'Goodnight, Nick,' I said softly. 'I'll see you in the morning.'

6

The next day dawned glorious and sunny and the forecast was for high temperatures. My head felt a little fuzzy but once we'd had breakfast, which Nick was thankfully quiet throughout, I was back to my usual cheery self. On our way to pick up the bus which was laid on specially to take trippers to Cowaramup, we browsed in some of the gift shops, where there were some wonderful hand-painted silks, fine paintings and pottery, and clothes made from hemp.

I could have whiled away the time for a lot longer but Nick was eager to be off so I had to quickly make up my mind about a hat. I finally decided upon one which was a cross between a drover's hat and a straw boater but suited me rather well I thought, and at least covered up my hair which I tended to think of as corkscrew hair now!

Once arrived at Cowaramup we were greeted with the gift of a wine glass engraved with Margaret River Wine Festival Tasting, etched on the side. I thought I'd keep it as a memento. Then Nick bought us a couple of foam pouches suspended on a neck tape so the glass could nestle in there leaving your hands free — I suppose in order to pour more wine.

'How come every one doesn't get completely plastered?'

'Don't know,' replied Nick. 'You have to give in a voucher each time you taste. I think you're only allowed so many per hour, but it's very laid back. No-one comes here to get plastered; it's a family event. A day out — not a booze up.'

I felt suitably chastened.

Dotted around the fields were lots of different gazebos all bearing banners stating their logos and the name of the vineyard. Already there was the aroma of food cooking and I noticed a couple of larger marquees where food was being prepared. There was a stream between two fields with a linking bridge for people to saunter across as the mood took them, and there were two large music stands set up, with ballads playing in the first field and, what sounded like heavy rock, in the second.

It soon became apparent that Nick had come to network. He was soon chatting to the music fraternity and helping here and there with equipment. The Fusion lasted from ten till six with non-stop music so I guessed there would be plenty of musicians around. I saw Jo together with Paddy and some other faces I recognised from Perth but didn't disturb them, as they looked pretty busy.

I wondered whether Jo, with the memorable catch in her voice, would be singing today. I hoped so. I hovered around in Nick's shadow for a while, and to be fair Nick did introduce me as a mate looking for her dad. At first I found this slightly demeaning, as though I'd somehow managed to drop my father out of my pocket on the crowd. On the whole though the musicians expressed polite interest, but again no one had heard of my dad.

I wandered around by myself for a while. Nick was into heavy conversations. Asking questions like, 'Who's representing you now?' and 'How many gigs are you signed up for?' They were questions I thought he was better asking alone.

The atmosphere was relaxed. Groups of people were wandering about taking in the ambience, tasting the wine, chatting and listening to the music. All in all a very pleasant way to while away the hours. Some of the stalls were selling vinegars and local oils, others selling soaps and herbal remedies. There were hats on sale too, and collapsible chairs and of course the all important water.

I didn't start tasting the wine until noon. The crowds were quite thick by this time. There were children with their faces painted like Micky Mouse or tigers. Young couples, old couples;

gangs of teenagers, looking as though they were here to enjoy themselves not cause trouble; hippy looking people and groups of women who could have been woman's institute members. It really was an eclectic mix. But above all they seemed to be smiling, laid back and living in the moment. I could think of worse places to be and decided I should live in the moment too.

Briefly, I caught sight of Natasha. She was kitted out in a T-shirt with Bradford Wines emblazoned across it, and was surrounded by would-be wine connoisseurs standing at least three deep. I started to make my way over to say hello, but suddenly an arm grabbed me from behind and a hand pushed my hat over my eyes. 'Hi ya,' said Nick softly in my ear. 'What's a gorgeous looking female like you doing all on her own in a place like this?'

'She's wine tasting and soaking up the sun,' I answered all thoughts of catching up with Natasha driven from my brain.

'I've bought us some veggie burgers. You'll love them.' He led me back to a leafy space between the back of the music marquee and a friendly eucalyptus tree. A blanket had been spread out and we sat cross legged, facing each other, sipping our wine and tucking into the veggie burgers, which I had to admit were very good.

'That filled a gap,' I said licking my fingers.

Nick stared at me intently.

'What's wrong?'

'I'm looking at your face.'

'What's wrong with my face?'

'Nothing. Absolutely nothing.'

Wow! It was an old one maybe, but none the less powerful for that.

Taking full advantage of the fact that I was momentarily completely stunned, Nick leaned forward across the small gap of blanket that separated us and kissed me full on the lips.

Our bodies weren't touching. I could have pulled back. I should have pulled back. But I didn't. I was conscious of the sun playing on my shoulders, some kind of Australian outback music strumming on in the background; the murmurings of the crowd and the smells of griddles when they got too hot. I was aware of Nick's lips on mine, of the shiver running from my head to my heart then on through my body to a place deep inside my heart that was normally only mine and Andy's.

Andy! My eyes flew open. What was I doing, what was Nick doing? I'd explained to him, I only wanted a friend. I'd told him and he'd said he understood. And here I was allowing the goal posts to be moved.

I wondered if the shock showed on my face. If it did Nick ignored it and traced a finger down the side of my nose. 'Don't look so scared. It was only a kiss. It's all your fault anyway. You shouldn't be so irresistible.'

The song, like the kiss had ended and as though on cue, Nick sprung to his feet. 'You might want to hear this,' he threw over his shoulder before disappearing round the side of the tent.

Still feeling slightly disorientated I followed him.

He'd grabbed a mic and jumped on to the makeshift stage.

'Hi everyone,' he started into the mic. 'I can see you're all enjoying yourselves out there. It's a great event isn't it?'

There were a few murmurings from the throng.

'Well, isn't it?' he insisted. This time the crowd agreed more audibly, and Nick gave the smile of someone who knew he didn't have to try too hard to have everyone like him. 'Seriously folks, we've got a great programme for you as you know, but before we get started again there's just a question I'd like to put to you. Does anyone know of a Bradley Williams? . . . He's a musical guy. In his forties, used to play piano and bass guitar — song writer too — sounds like a talented guy.'

He paused and looked round the

crowd. 'Well, don't all shout at once
. . . No? OK. We know he's lived or
worked in these parts. So if you know
him, or of him, perhaps you'd ask him
to get in touch with me, because I know
someone who'd love to see him. Oh
. . . I'm Nick Packer by the way, if you
don't know me already.'

There was a faint round of applause
and Nick grinned again, that particularly attractive grin of his, before
leaping down from the stage and
handing the mic to a lady with bright
pink hair who was obviously waiting to
go on stage.

'What d'you think of that?' he asked
me.

'Thanks,' I said my heart beating
wildly. 'That was great.'

I took up vigil after that, hovering
near the side of the stage in the forlorn
hope that someone would come over
and say that yes, they knew Brad
Williams and here was his address. It
didn't happen.

By the end of the afternoon I had to

admit to myself that it wasn't going to happen either. But, I reasoned to myself, not everyone would have heard Nick's speech. All those trying wines, of which there were many, would have only heard the distant mumblings of an announcement of some kind.

But, went a counter voice inside me, most of those who'd come to hear the music would have already established their pitches near the music stand — surely someone there would have heard of him and shown some interest? I had to face it, this had been my best chance yet and all it had produced was a big fat nothing.

I consoled myself by sipping at my wine and listening in on Nick's conversations, the subject matter of which had now switched to the Aria Awards, which were held in October at the Sydney Super Dome. Briefly I toyed with the idea of staying till next January — nearly a year away, travelling to Sydney and searching for my father all over again at the Aria Awards.

Apparently, there would be a cross section of Australian musicians, singers and songwriters there, from hardcore rock 'n' rollers to pop singers and country crooners. Maybe in Sydney I'd have a chance of finding him.

Only that was a year away! I couldn't stay in Australia for a year, could I? But I couldn't just give up either. I'd only been here a week and even this soon it felt as though I was running out of options. Surely, if I couldn't find my dad here with all the help I was getting, I couldn't find him anywhere and Andy was right, I needed my head examined for ever thinking I could.

After applauding loudly to Jo's plaintive rendition of a song about lost love, mainly because of the singer — not the song, I glanced at my watch. It was coming up for five o'clock and a slow steady trickle of people was making their way to the exit. Suddenly I wanted to be one of them.

My shoulders felt slightly sore and I was aware of a persistent pain at the back of my eyes. And I was fed up with Nick's full on or full off attention. Right now he was at the centre of a laughing group of beautiful people looking as fresh as a daisy and as though he could make a night of it.

Just then I caught his eye and a momentary flash of irritation showed in his face. He came over to my side.

'If it's OK with you, Nick, I think I'll go home on the bus now,' I said. 'I've had a great day, but to tell you the truth I can feel the beginnings of a headache — so if you don't mind . . . '

Immediately Nick was all smiling concern. 'Course not, babe — no worries.'

He put an arm round my shoulders and gave me a painful squeeze. 'Probably had too much sun,' he said as I winced. 'That and too much wine . . . '

And maybe, too much of you, I thought to myself but didn't say. Of course I didn't.

He offered to take me to the bus, but

I refused as it was right outside the exit and it was, I suspected, with relief that he turned back to his friends to do some 'catching up'. I glanced back when I reached the exit, noticing that once again he was the centre of attention.

Once on the bus I began to feel a lot better. I decided that after I'd picked up my e-mail I'd eat a small meal at the hotel and have an early night.

7

The Internet café was open with only two or three others sitting at computers. I quickly logged on to find I had three e-mails waiting for me. One was from Mum, one from a contact Nick thought might have had news of my dad, and one from Andy. Two seconds later I was starting at the screen in disbelief.

Dear Caro, wrote Andy. *Please let me know you're OK. I do worry about you. I hope you've managed to find news of your dad. I'm sorry for being a jerk. I miss you more than I ever expected. You seem so out of reach. Love Andy.*

This was a new Andy. *Love Andy? Sorry? Miss you?* And most amazing of all — *You seem so out of reach.* From *Andy*, this was almost poetry. He was a 'see you', sort of guy. He never called me 'babe' or 'gorgeous' or — what else was it Nick had said not less than two hours ago — 'irresistible'. No, not Andy.

Andy never said anything he didn't mean. He was missing me, not just in an *it would be nice to see Caro* kind of way, but in a gut wrenching *how can I live without her* way. I read the words over and over again. And he put love — love. He would have thought about that. It wasn't a word that sprang easily to his lips.

Andy, I tapped back rapidly before I could change my mind. *Thanks for the message. No luck yet I'm afraid, but not giving up just yet even though I feel discouraged and am missing you so very much. You know my reasons for coming, but I'm sorry too, for upsetting you, and not giving you time to get used to the idea of my trip.*

I only read it through once. Then I deleted *so very much*, because that was actually a lie. Although he was never far from my thoughts, I couldn't be missing him that much or I would never have allowed the guilty kiss with Nick to happen.

I put my fingers up to my hot cheeks and wished I didn't keep reliving that kiss quite so often.

The other e-mails proved not to be so interesting. The contact didn't know my dad, and Mum's message was determinedly cheerful but full of motherly caution regarding, 'not taking lifts from strangers or going back to their flats for coffee'. *I know you're sensible really*, she put. *But on holiday it's easy to relax your guard*.

I slowly walked back through the town, which was full of families and tourists and after a shower and a modest meal, went back to my room to do some serious thinking.

It must have been at about eleven-thirty, that I heard Nick tap on my door.

'You awake, Caro?' he asked softly. I resisted the impulse to snore loudly and obviously. Instead I just lay there chastely in my dark room, hardly daring to breathe, until he went away.

What did you say your dad's name was?' It was five days since I'd come back from Margaret River and I was sitting next to Jo in a posh hairdressing salon very near to the Breakie Bar — I'd learned to call it 'breakie' now — where I worked mornings. I'd been rather down in the dumps since the Wine Festival because it seemed as though my quest had ground to a halt.

Also I'd had no further contact from Andy which, I reasoned to myself, was understandable, as he was busy, and anyway we'd hardly been in daily contact in the recent past. I had hoped however that he might have responded to my last e-mail with a quick 'still missing you' or something . . . Anything really, would have done.

'My dad's name,' I said, hardly able to believe any of my Australian acquaintances didn't have his name burnt into their memories by now, 'is Bradley Williams.'

Jo stared at me as though wondering whether or not to continue. My heart rate began to quicken. 'Come on, you can tell me,' I encouraged. 'Look, I never really knew him. If he's dead or something, I won't freak out, I promise.'

'It's not that. It's just that, well, I'm not sure, but it seems too much of a coincidence to be true . . . But it might not be your dad, you know. There's probably more than one Brad Williams?'

'Well, if you know of one, it'll be one more than I've heard of. Come on — tell me.' I was nearly dying of impatience now.

'It was the photo, really,' said Jo. 'You know the one you showed me? I know it was out of date but something about the nose . . . and then there was the tattoo?'

'The tattoo? Oh, the anchor — on his wrist? Millions of people have an anchor on their wrist.'

'That's what I thought. Anyway, last time I talked to home, I asked my mum if she knew anyone called Brad Williams . . . '

'And?'

'She said she and my dad used to have a neighbour, Rita, who had a boyfriend called Brad, but she couldn't remember the surname, but she thought it was something with a Welsh sound. Roberts or Jones — possibly Williams? They've lost touch now, but the funny thing is — he's the one I was thinking about who knew a lot about wine and has a daughter in England? I met him a couple of times at my parents' barbecues. Apparently he only spoke about this daughter that one time I was there, he'd probably had one too many wines. Never would speak about her again.'

By now I'd lost interest in whatever it was Nick had told them to do to my hair, my eyes in the mirror were fastened on Jo's face. 'Well, where is he? What's he like? How do I find him?'

'That's the trouble. Last time they heard about him he was in the Barossa Valley just outside Adelaide — my parents live in Adelaide — I told you that already, didn't I?'

'Barossa Valley? Never heard of it.'

'It's where the best Australian wine grapes are grown?'

'I thought that was Margaret River. Well, never mind all that. Who did he work for? Can I phone them?'

My voice had become an excited squeak and the other clients were staring at me as though I was something out of a zoo.

'I asked my mum to look in the phone book, but she said she couldn't possibly phone all the B Williams in there? Rita and he split up long ago and anyway Rita's moved away . . . From what Mum could remember he worked for himself — used to drive a tour bus from Adelaide to the Barossa Valley? But she can't remember which one.'

'How long ago was this?'

'About three or four years?'

'Right.'

Suddenly I was back to earth with a bump. Suppose Jo and her mum were right, and this Bradley Williams was my dad, how was I going to trace him? It would be no easier looking for someone with a knowledge of wine in the Barossa Valley than searching for a musician at a music festival in Sydney; or even, come to that, at a celebration of wine and music at Margaret River.

The impossibility of the task ahead threatened to overwhelm me, but I still knew I'd go. I'd take a flight to Adelaide. I'd find somewhere to stay in the Barossa Valley and once again I'd start looking, even if it were for a needle in a haystack.

'So you actually spoke to him? What was he like? Did he look like me? Was he nice?'

Jo laughed. 'Look, we don't even know it was him, do we? But yes, from what I remember he was nice, just a regular bloke, you know? I didn't take a lot of notice really. I mean he was one of my parents' friends. Just the daughter thing sort of stuck.

'The idea of him sending a present

once a year? I wondered how the daughter felt about it?'

'Well, now you know,' I took a shaky breath. 'I took it for granted until it stopped happening.' My voice ended on a wobble.

'Are you excited about tonight?'

Obviously Jo had picked up on the sheer impossibility of the task ahead of me, the hopelessness of my mood and was adroitly changing the subject. Even so, I could tell by her voice that the thought of attending the new Top Venue night club that Nick, as a minor celebrity, had been invited to open, was a dream come true. Me? Well, I wasn't so sure.

For a start I was vaguely uneasy at the idea of Nick springing the surprise on me that I was to be his 'date' for the evening and that he'd arranged for me to have a 'make over' at his expense especially for the occasion. He thought I'd be overjoyed but somehow, nightclubs have never been my scene. I'm more a running track kind of girl.

Nevertheless I felt I owed him something, so here I was being straightened and highlighted, having a manicure and a make up session; and question-mark-Jo, as one of Nick's bright new finds, was having the same treatment alongside me.

Jo did have an amazing voice though, question mark at the end of every sentence or not. The boyfriend had either been dropped along the wayside or had been left deliberately to lurk in the shadows, because I'd heard no mention of him since we'd come back from Margaret River.

8

I hadn't seen too much of Nick over the
last few days either. He'd been busy. I'd
also been busy and quite content to
spend my spare time after work surfing
the net on all the musical sites looking
for any mention of my dad. I'd spent
time with Jenny and Paul and taken
them out to a nice restaurant as a thank
you for everything they had done and
were continuing to do for me.

I was glad to get back to the Breakie
Bar. I'd missed the other staff and also
my regulars.

The hair straightening guy had nearly
finished his job now and the top layer of
my hair was several shades lighter — a
sort of strawberry blonde, whereas the
underneath although still brownish red
was sleek and shiny. The whole effect
was one of sophistication, obviously
much better suited to a night spot

opening than a running track.

I thanked the hairdresser who seemed quite blasé at the miracle he'd just performed on my corkscrew hair. Then it was on to the make-up girl and pretty soon my freckles had been obliterated, my eyes looked twice their normal size and my lips looked luscious and full.

'You look stunning,' said a Jo, who I had difficulty recognising.

'So do you.'

She did, but somehow with the introduction of glamorous make up and a hair do to match I felt she'd lost a little of her fresh innocent appeal. 'Wow, one night of sheer sophistication, eh? How are we going to face tomorrow?'

'With panda eyes and a hangover probably,' said a voice behind me. Nick had sneaked in without my noticing. His eyes as he looked at us both were mildly calculating, then suddenly his expression relaxed. 'Terrific!' he pronounced. 'You look great — both of you. Got to get my skates on now. I'll see you around ten at the club. Don't worry, you only have to give your name at the door, they'll let you in, it's all arranged.'

And he'd gone. As quickly as that.

Jo's expression was slightly glassy as though she'd just been permitted a glimpse of a demi-god. I exchanged glances with the fellow who'd worked the hair straightening miracle. His expression said Jo was a hero worshipper with no hope — but then, he hadn't heard her sing.

'Snap out of it, Jo,' I said. 'I think you and I will be seeing quite a lot of each other tonight, and not much of Nick — he'll be networking.'

Momentarily Jo looked embarrassed, then when she realised I was smiling — confused. 'You are his girlfriend, aren't you?'

'No,' I said. 'I don't know what gave you that idea. But no way.'

'Well, that's what he calls you. He says you're his English girlfriend?'

That gave me food for thought. 'Does

he indeed? Well, I don't know why. We're only friends, I promise you.'

'I've seen the way he looks at you. Perhaps he has plans to change that?' suggested Jo with a smile that said it all.

It was a Saturday evening and Jenny and Paul had planned to go to a friend's birthday. They had invited me to go along but when I explained about the nightclub opening Jenny had shrugged and said, 'Well, you're only young once. I expect our friend's birthday would be pretty tame compared to a nightclub opening.'

I didn't know quite how to answer that one. I'd picked up the vibes that Jenny did not like what little she knew of Nick Packer but I resented the way she seemed to have turned overnight from my friend to my disapproving older sister. And as a guest staying in her house it was hard to know how to react sometimes. I decided not to mention Jo and her Barossa Valley story, in case she poured cold water over that one too.

When I'd arrived back complete with straight hair and made-over face, Paul had whistled in a complimentary fashion and even Jenny had done a double take. 'You look great,' she admitted. 'Not like you, but yeah, terrific!'

I thanked them for their vote of confidence and mumbled that as it was to be a late night I would probably take up Jo's offer to stay over with her.

'Right,' said Jenny, as though it wasn't right at all. Then, 'Have fun . . . See you tomorrow.'

I wore the strappy little number that I'd become especially fond of, now I had a bit of a golden tan. Jo looked great in something turquoise and floaty and as we arrived at the club a couple of cameras flashed. It made me feel like minor royalty and I couldn't help smiling.

Before long the club was heaving with bodies. I wasn't as impressed as Jo was by the guest list, they were all body beautifuls but still strangers to me. We helped ourselves to some free champagne and a few nibbles and pretty soon we were separated and chatting to the other guests. Because of my job, I suppose, I find it pretty easy to chat to all types, but it didn't take long before I was back on to my old hobby horse of, 'I'm looking for my dad. Have you heard of a guy called Brad Williams?'

I was able to do this now without a shadow of embarrassment. After all if they looked bored it was quite simple to change the subject to the wonders of Australia — in particular the wonderful beaches of Perth.

However, as I had suspected, most of those attending were well under forty so I wasn't surprised that none of the people I spoke to had any recollection of my dad.

About an hour after we arrived, the club owner took a microphone and introduced Nick, stressing how much influence he'd had in the music business and in particular the shaping of Dee's career. ' . . . and as we know she's gone on to do fabulously well in UK.'

Nick then said a few words indicating that although their deciding to end their partnership had been mutual, well — enough said — he wished Dee all the luck in the world. He then sadly looked into the middle distance in an 'if only' sort of way, but quickly brought himself back to the present and declared the club to be officially open.

As performances went it was brilliant. Everyone was on Nick's side.

'Poor Nick,' said Jo, equally affected. 'I really think he's a lot more sensitive than he pretends.'

'Do you?' was all I could manage.

9

It was to be at least an hour later that Nick caught up with us again and then it was just to spend about five minutes asking us how we felt he'd come across, and off he went again working the crowd as though his life depended on it. In his line of business that was what it was all about. And after all, wasn't I very grateful for it?

He'd managed to promote my dad's name in the musical world of Perth as well as at Margaret River. I mustn't lose sight of that fact. Without him where would I be? No better off certainly. And I wouldn't be able to cross Margaret River and Perth off my list of places my father could be, because that was exactly what I was going to do, I realised. My next target was the Barossa Valley, and if that turned out to be a non starter, then it would be Sydney.

Someone, somewhere, had to have heard of my dad!

By two o'clock in the morning I was bored out of my brain. I enjoy dancing as much as the next person and Jo and I had danced with various partners and with each other. But whereas Jo knew all the personalities being gossiped about between our forays on to the dance floor, I knew none of them and found it difficult to keep up with the conversation without yawning.

Eventually Nick found his way to my side again and grabbed me for a couple of dances. He was a good dancer, it had to be said and once again, I had his attention — full on. So I played the game, danced and smiled, flirted a little I suppose, all the time aware that this was another performance for both of us. Well, that was OK. I owed him.

The cameras flashed again as we left the club. Nick had his arm round me, his face very close to mine and Jo was on his other side beaming into the camera lens. I hoped Nick would be happy with the pictures, because I didn't doubt that he'd set them up.

Jo and I slept in the twin beds in the spare room of Nick's parents' flat that night. Nick slept next door in his own room.

I felt like a fish out of water, and I'd never missed Andy so much.

The next morning as we sat together with coffee and the Sunday papers I found myself telling Jenny how much I was missing Andy and that I didn't really care for Nick or his lifestyle after all.

'Something about him last night really got on my nerves,' I admitted a trifle shamefaced. 'But the thing is, I feel a bit guilty about the way I've been using him.'

Jenny's eyebrows shot up to her hairline. 'You — using him?' she squeaked. 'I don't think there's much chance of that. I ask you, what harm is he doing to his reputation having a gorgeous English girl like you on his arm? I'd say you were a very good piece of PR for him. I'm just glad you've seen him for what he is — a charming, good-looking go-getter, at least you won't get your heart broken now.'

She put her arm round my shoulders and gave me a squeeze and feeling a lot better than I had in a long time, I told her about my conversation with Jo and my proposed trip to the Barossa Valley. 'I only need to book my flight,' I said. 'Jo's mum has already offered to put me up for a couple of nights.'

To my surprise and relief Jenny was enthusiastic about the idea. 'In fact I can fix up the flight for you through work. If you go on the wine tour, you can ask around. Speak to the driver. They often remember other drivers working for the opposition.'

As good as her word Jenny got straight on to her computer, and picked up a cheap cancellation for me. I rang Jo on her mobile and she confirmed that her mum would be delighted to have me stay for a couple of nights.

Monday morning, bright and early

found me at the Breakie Bar again.

As always the morning went quickly and it wasn't until I was clearing up that I realised I was ready for a break. Then I heard a voice I recognised and it sounded rather cross.

'There you are!' He was more than cross, he was furious. Still handsome, but furious all the same.

'Hi, Nick,' I said. 'Bit early for you, isn't it? Anyway, how did you know I worked here?'

'The same way as everyone else in Perth will know,' he replied shaking a newspaper in my face.

'OK calm down,' I said taking in the half page photo that had been snapped as we left the nightclub.

'So what's the problem?' I said examining the photo. 'Quite good of you and I don't look too bad — not awful enough for you to be so angry about anyway.'

'No, the write up — read the write up.'

Obediently I read the write up. It said

118

that Nick Packer was helping his English girlfriend to trace her father . . .

I looked up. 'Great, I never thought of putting it in the papers. That's really good advertising for you and me.'

Nick still looked thunderous.

'I don't see what's wrong with that,' I said.

'Go on,' said Nick in icy tones. 'Read the rest.'

'*However it seems that's as far as his help goes. I can reveal that Carolyn Williams is not staying with Nick in his Northbridge flat*, it's not your flat anyway,' I commented. 'It belongs to your parents.' Then I read on, '*And she's making ends meet and is funding her expenses by working in the Breakie Bar in Perth city* centre. Well, what's wrong with that?'

Nick looked as though he was about to burst a blood vessel. 'You didn't tell me! That's what's wrong with it. You went sneaking around behind my back.'

Trying to stay calm, I folded the paper and handed it back to him. 'Well,

I'm sorry, Nick, but I don't have to tell you everything. Anyway who cares? It's nobody else's business.'

Nick looked sulky as well as angry. 'That's not the point. It makes me look like a skinflint. They obviously think we have a relationship going — and well, this makes me look a complete idiot.'

'You're doing that quite well all by yourself . . . And why would they think we have a relationship going anyway? I've certainly never given anyone that idea.'

He looked at me through narrowed eyes. 'Last night you danced with me in a very intimate fashion.'

Intimate fashion — how old fashioned! I laughed. 'Come off it, Nick, it was just a dance and it was part of your performance wasn't it? You're 'look at me aren't I the popular one' performance? I was just playing along to keep your public happy. That was the idea, wasn't it?'

Suddenly his expression turned to that of a thwarted, spoiled child. 'Who d'you think you are? You've made enough use of me, haven't you? You've used my contacts, used my help, and this is all the gratitude I get.'

My patience was wearing thin now. 'Oh for goodness sake you sound like a Victorian heroine. We used each other. Well — didn't we? You were feeling a bit low after being booted out by Dee. You didn't want to show up in your home town without an adoring female in tow, and if you could be Nick the hero involved in helping her find her old man so well and good. It would be an added interest factor. And if there was rather a nice story that came out just as you opened the new nightspot, well, even better. Good for me too. I think we can say we used each other. But if I choose to work in the Breakie Bar, that's my decision. I have to pay my own way. That's the way I've been brought up.

'And if your friend, the journalist, found that out, well done him, but it's hardly story of the week! And now if you'll excuse me . . . ' I squirted his hand, which was resting on the table I'd just been clearing, with soapy liquid and applied my cloth with a brisk rubbing action. He withdrew his hand quickly and when I next looked up, he'd gone.

10

In the train on the way back to Jenny and Paul's, I heaved a sigh of relief. I didn't know whether I'd ever see Nick again or whether he'd still regard me as a friend and I found that I didn't care much either way. Oh he was nice enough, I supposed, nice, but shallow. I wondered whether I was becoming shallow too. Maybe, normally I wouldn't have latched on to him quite so quickly, I told myself. Somehow with finding my father being my number one priority my normal rules for living had become blurred along the way.

But it seemed that surprises that day were still not over. Later, when I let myself into the cool of the house with the key Jenny had given me, I felt the hairs on the back of my neck stand up. After the bright sunlight outside, the interior with it's drawn blinds seemed especially gloomy. Silent too, but with a strange sort of expectancy in the quiet.

'Hi,' I called walking through to the dining area because Jenny had told me she'd be in. Then I stopped on the threshold, staring in disbelief as a tall broad shouldered figure pushed back a chair and got to his feet.

'Andy!' I whispered only half believing my eyes.

In two strides he was across the room, then just before taking me in his arms, he changed his mind, stopped and looked at me questioningly.

My heart was beating like a drum. Same crooked smiled, same intense dark eyes. Hair a bit too long? Probably. Clothes a little creased? Undoubtedly. But it was Andy — the guy I'd left behind. The guy I'd like to spend the rest of my life with.

Behind him on the table I could see a copy of the same newspaper Nick had thrust at me this morning. Oh no!

The best form of defence is attack so they say.

'What on earth are you doing here? Why didn't you tell me you were coming?'

'Thought I'd surprise you,' said Andy. 'Seems I did.' He indicated towards the newspaper.

'Oh, that,' I said carelessly. 'That's nothing. Doesn't mean a thing.'

'Doesn't mean a thing,' repeated Andy tonelessly. 'Well, well. You could have fooled me. I'd say it meant that for someone whose main objective was to find her father you're hanging on entirely the wrong arm. Several years too young an arm for a start.'

'I've already explained to you about Nick, he's got contacts in the music business. Anyway, we've just had a row.'

If anything Andy's expression became even more frozen. 'Row as in 'lover's tiff?'

'No. Row as in 'you're a pain in the neck — get off my case'!'

Andy rubbed a tired hand across his eyes and took a couple of unsteady steps back to the table. It was only then

I noticed Jenny was sitting outside under the patio roof, obviously intending to be tactful.

'I'm sorry, Andy,' I said because suddenly I was sorry, because this should have been a wonderful moment and somehow it had all gone wrong. 'You should have told me you were coming. You look so tired, when did you arrive?'

'Half-an-hour ago,' said Jenny who, it appeared, judged it to be safe to come in. 'He's booked into a basic hotel right near your Breakie Bar, but he hasn't been there yet, he came straight here from the airport.'

For some reason this made me feel like crying, but I didn't.

'I wish you'd told me, Andy,' I repeated. 'I've arranged to go to Adelaide tomorrow.'

'Oh great,' said Andy as though the opposite were true. 'With or without lover boy in attendance?'

I felt a sudden flash of annoyance. 'It's a single ticket, always was a single ticket and will continue to be a single ticket. Get that through your head.'

'I'm sorry, I didn't mean that. It's just, well, now I've caught up on the workload at home, I thought I'd come over to help.'

'It's a bit late for that. I've already made the arrangements. I'm staying with Jo's mum — and before you ask — Jo is a girl . . . If you really want to help you can cover for me at the Breakie Bar for two days. They're really struggling to find the staff. That would be what I call practical help.'

In the end, because of the jet lag, Jenny and I drove Andy back to his hotel in Perth. Jenny offered to put him up but he wouldn't hear of it; said we both needed time to think.

Personally I thought time to think was the one thing we didn't need. What I, at least, needed was for him to sweep me into his arms and declare his undying love for me, say he forgave me for everything I may, or may not have done wrong. But no, that wasn't Andy.

Andy was deliberate and had to mean what he said. Andy was not shallow. Not nice either, I thought to myself. Then I amended that to — not nice just at the moment, because he was tired, disappointed and jealous. In retrospect it was probably best that we had a bit of time to figure things out, and perhaps it might do him the tiniest bit of good to feel the tiniest bit jealous. There you are, I was shallow without a doubt.

I kissed Andy very briefly goodbye. It had to be brief because there was no parking outside the hotel.

'Look — I'll come with you to Adelaide.'

'You can't. I told you, Jenny's got me a special deal. I'm staying with Jo's mum and I'll only be gone two days anyway.'

'You don't want me to come?'

Oh, I did, I did want him to come!

'Not really — no. You'd just complicate the issue.'

'Fine.'

'Fine!'

I told him I'd text him, but I didn't say I loved him. It seemed best not to somehow.

11

The Barossa Valley Tour Jenny had fixed for me wasn't until my second day in Adelaide. Linda, as Jo's mum introduced herself at the airport, turned out to be a typically warm hearted Australian, brushing my thanks for all she was doing for me, aside.

'Nonsense,' she said. 'Jo spoke highly of you as soon as she met you, and it seems you've spoken a deal of sense to her? It's funny how she'll listen to someone in her own age group and not to her own mother, but then I suppose I was the same at her age?'

There it was, the question mark thing again. It must run in the family. I was glad but slightly surprised that I'd 'spoken a deal of sense' to Jo. All I'd said as far as I was aware was not to take Nick Packer too seriously and to stay focused on the music side of things, and I didn't think she'd listened at the time.

Linda took me to where her car was parked and we set off to Adelaide city centre where we were to late lunch at a 'dinky little Italian place' she knew. En route we had a fast city tour with a running commentary from Linda.

'The inner city is a square mile built round Light Square. Colonel Light was the guy who planned the city then surrounded it with open parklands because the cannon's range from the cover of the trees wouldn't reach and therefore damage the city? All the school kids are taught about Colonel Light?'

I sat back and admired the wide streets, built wide for carts and bullocks to turn easily. Linda pointed out Government House and the Art Gallery in North Terrace, but I must admit I didn't find the buildings or the city itself at first glance, as attractive as Perth on this whistle stop tour.

The 'dinky' Italian place turned out

to be very small, very friendly and very reasonable. I insisted on buying lunch for us both and Linda plied me with questions about Jo and Nick Packer, and did I really think Jo stood a chance in the music business.

I started to feel hot and flustered. 'I don't know what Jo's told you, but I know nothing about the music business. The only thing I do know is that my father was in it, but no-one seems to have heard of him so obviously he wasn't well known enough to have been considered successful . . . '

Linda looked a little disappointed.

'But Jo has a good voice,' I went on hurriedly, 'and more important — there's something about her voice you remember. She has a sort of catch in it that you can recognise and the second or third time you hear it you think, 'oh yeah, that's the girl with the catch in her voice' . . . ' My voice trailed off into nothing because it wasn't much to offer, but Linda brightened considerably.

'So, you don't think Nick Packer is just stringing her along? You really think he's got hopes for her?'

'Let me put it like this. I don't think Nick would waste time on anyone he didn't think had talent or was tough enough to see it through.'

For a long moment Linda held my gaze. 'You don't like him, do you?'

I sighed. 'It's not that I don't like him. It's just that he's a businessman and he treats people as commodities. But Jo's a sensible girl. She may have had a bit of a crush on him at first, but now I think she's realised that her best way forward is to show him she's serious about singing and she's professional in her approach. I think after Dee, Nick will try not to mix personal relationships with the business side of things.'

Linda gave me a sidelong glance. 'I expect he tried it on with you though?'

'I made it very clear from the beginning that I wasn't interested,' I said. Then I looked away knowing that wasn't strictly true and I had been very tempted.'

'I have a boyfriend in London,' I went on. 'Well actually no, he's not in London now. He's just flown out to Perth. He couldn't come before because of work commitments, but he came as soon as he could.'

'Wow!' said Linda. 'He must love you very much, to come so far just to be with you?'

'Yes,' I said looking away again and blinking rapidly, 'I think he must.'

Jo's mum and dad lived in the eastern suburbs, in a leafy street full of elegant houses, set against a backdrop of rolling hills.

I wanted to ask exactly which house it was that the man who might have been my dad had lived in, but I was scared to broach the subject.

I needn't have worried, once Linda had shown me my room, which was beautifully decorated in blue and white, she called me down for a drink, and opened a large photograph album.

I thought at first that I was in for a trip down memory lane with Jo at various ages in cute party dresses but no, Linda knew exactly what she was searching for.

'Here,' she said. 'This is it. Taken four years ago. It's not terribly clear but this is Rita and that's her boyfriend at the time — Brad. What d'you think? D'you think it could be him?'

Placing my old photo next to it, I scrutinised the photo. It was strange because the photo did remind me of someone — it did look familiar in some way. The noses in the two photos looked similar but the picture caught a side view, which meant that I couldn't see the expression in the eyes. His hair was longish too and looked fairly grey. It might be him, it might not be. It was impossible to say.

'Well as you know I was too young to remember him, but it does look as though they could be the same man, and his name was Brad you say, even if you can't remember the surname? Can

I take this photo with me tomorrow on the tour, maybe someone will recognise him and tell me a little more?'

'Sure you can. The other thing I've remembered is Brad used a particular tea room to take his clients to, he had a deal with them, you know it was part of the price — a cream tea thrown in. It was in the main street of Hahndorf where the German settlement was set up. They may remember him there and know where he's gone to.'

I made a note of this, and glanced at the other questions I wanted to ask Linda.

'Do you remember him saying that he came from Perth?'

Linda looked less confident. 'I think so. But you know how it is when someone puts an idea in your mind, it's easy to convince yourself — so I'm not really sure.'

'Oh.' I was a little disappointed but tried not to let it show. 'Did he mention the music industry much? Will it be worth my trying any music venues when I come back to Adelaide after the tour?'

Linda looked vague. 'To tell you the truth, although he told Jo she could hold a tune and if she had a lucky break she might get somewhere, he sounded pretty disillusioned about making any more money out of music himself. He did have a hit you know? But he didn't write or sing under his own name.'

This was news. 'Why on earth not?'

'Something to do with his family not approving?'

'Not approving? That's mad.'

'I know. He was pretty cagey, wouldn't tell us the name he'd had his hit under or what it was. We never could get to the bottom of it. But then, we didn't try particularly. As far as we were concerned he was a friend of a neighbour's who's now moved away. Anyway Rita broke up with him. Said he was too much of a free spirit to tie down.'

My heart turned over at the phrase 'free spirit'.

Then Linda smiled. 'He was a lovely man, though. We all liked him. But he was a wanderer. Australia's full of them. You're on the right track though, if you want a feel for what he used to do at least for a couple of seasons, going on the tour will do that. You'll travel the same roads he travelled and see the same scenes, if nothing else, maybe it will make you feel closer to him.'

I went to bed that night feeling just a little more hopeful.

★   ★   ★

The next morning bright and early, Linda dropped me at the coach terminal from where the tour was due to start.

Bruce, the designated driver had a friendly face and was obviously quite happy to spend five minutes or so chatting whilst waiting for the others to turn up. Before I knew it, I'd confided in him my reason for being on the tour and shown him the photo Linda had lent me.

'Sorry, can't say that I recognise him, but that doesn't mean anything. We get a fair few drivers through here . . . Ask around in Hahndorf though, shopkeepers there might remember, it's quite a small place.'

Slightly encouraged I took a seat near the front and listened in a trance-like state as Bruce drove us out of Adelaide giving a commentary all the while until taking the Port Rush Road towards the Barossa Valley.

I learned that the graceful purple flowered trees that lined the streets were called Jacaranda trees and that Adelaide was once called city of the churches although now many had been altered into offices, boutiques and one even into a nightclub. I learned that the early settlers came from England, Germany, and Scotland, and that now the population had swollen to over a million.

A million people! What chance did I

have of finding even one person who'd heard of my dad? I felt despondent again. Then somehow, as we started to follow the river through the spectacular Torrens Gorge, my spirits started to lift. My dad's driven along this road, I thought to myself. He's driven along here and given out the same facts and figures as Bruce, probably even cracked the same jokes.

From then on I listened in earnest and gave myself over to enjoying the day and taking what I could from it. We went past some dairy and sheep farming communities although fruit farming seemed to be most popular. It all looked rather similar to the English countryside.

Then we came to Williamstown with its beautiful stone buildings. This was where the first German settlers came to in the 1850s and grapes and olives have been grown in the region since that time, Bruce informed us.

12

We stopped for some wine tasting and I discovered why it was I liked some Chardonnay wines and not others. The wine matured in oak barrels had an entirely different flavour to that of the wine matured in steel barrels, so I resolved in future to read the wine label and avoid those Chardonnay wines matured in oak.

If only the other things I'd come to find out were resolved so easily. By the time I'd enjoyed a tasty lunch at one of the winery restaurants, taken a stroll under the elm trees along Hahndorf's main street and cross examined most of the owners of the quaint craft shops in the area, I felt that I was getting nowhere.

Wearily, I made my way to the tea shop Linda had told me about and ordered tea and a scone. Guessing that most of the coach load would make the tea shop their first stop and the shop would therefore be busy, I'd left it till last deliberately. Sure enough when the waitress, maybe just a couple of years older than me, delivered my cream tea, I judged her to be relaxed enough to take an interest in my story. At first her expression remained blank and totally disinterested — then I handed her the photograph.

A flicker of recognition kindled in her eyes. 'Oh, you mean Brad,' she said.

I felt sick, dizzy and amazed. 'That's right,' I said. 'D'you know where he is?'

The waitress shrugged her shoulders. 'No, but I remember him. He was a laugh. Knew a lot about wine too. Don't know where he's gone, but he often spoke about the wines where he came from being better than anything in the Barossa Valley. Not to the clients, of course, but he did to us.'

'Did he say where he came from?'

'Margaret River.'

Bingo! I should have felt elated, but I

knew I was back to square one.

'You've no idea where he went to?'

'Sorry.'

'Well, thanks anyway,' I mumbled.

I drank half the tea, but somehow didn't fancy the cream scone after that.

★ ★ ★

That evening after a long talk with Linda, I decided to go back to Perth as planned. There seemed little point in staying in Adelaide. Brad Williams, if indeed it was he, had probably left the area by now. Might only have come here on a whim in the first place. Armed now with the knowledge that his music career had been under another name I would go back to Perth and if the trail was still as cold — then what? Give up, said a voice in my head. Enjoy the holiday with Andy. Go and watch whales, visit King's Park and the museums, go to Swan Valley for more wine tasting. Do all this with Andy. Then go home.

I stared hard at my mobile phone and thought back to the last e-mail message I'd had from Andy. '*You seem so out of reach*,' he'd said. And that's how my father seemed to me. Out of reach, out of touch, maybe dead. I shivered. I really didn't want it to end like this. I went back to fiddling with my phone and found a text message from Andy. When was I coming back to Perth? Had I had any luck? Please to ring him.

Try as I might I couldn't disguise the disappointment in my voice when I got through to him. 'I'm sorry, Andy,' I started. 'You were right, it's been a waste of time. When I get back to Perth we'll concentrate on having a good holiday. I've hardly seen Perth really. We'll do touristy things together.'

'Whatever you want,' said Andy against a background that was buzzing with a mix of conversation, music and laughter.

Suddenly I felt unreasonably jealous. There he was obviously sitting in some bar or restaurant having a good time and sounding disgracefully cheerful about the fact I'd come up with nothing. I hadn't expected abject sympathy exactly, but I'd expected a few words of comfort!

'I think we should just forget it and have a good time while you're out here — go and watch the whales or something, hire a car and go down the coast,' I reiterated. 'Then when you go home, I'll give it a bit longer I think, but not become so obsessed I promise. I'll just have to accept the fact that he's either dead or he just doesn't want to be found.'

I told him what time I'd be arriving back in Perth the next day then, because he didn't seem to have much to say, made the excuse that phoning on an English phone cost the earth out here and rang off.

Slowly, I packed my few belongings together and tried to rid myself of the feeling that Andy had sounded strange on the phone. Not strange as in ill or anything, just well — odd. It was something I couldn't quite put my finger on, almost as though he were reluctant to talk to me. But that didn't make any sense at all, did it?

13

'We're all going out tonight,' was the first thing Andy said to me when he and Jenny met me at the airport.

I'd only just recovered from the sight of him turning my heart over. Now it returned to beating at its normal rate, I realised that, actually, I'd rather like to spend the evening alone with Andy, maybe curled up together on a sofa somewhere.

I tried to summon the necessary enthusiasm. 'OK. But I'm really tired Andy, so let's not make it too late.'

Unusually, Andy seemed to be in a party mood. 'One thing I found out pretty fast is that Perth closes at seven.'

'That's a bit of an exaggeration,' said Jenny, and they both laughed.

It wasn't that funny. In fact I couldn't understand why they kept exchanging glances and laughing like a couple of hyenas, or perhaps it was just that I really wasn't in the mood.

Eventually Andy remembered to ask me about my trip, and I filled him in with the details I hadn't bothered with during our phone call the previous evening.

'Linda's really nice,' I finished, 'she's just like an older edition of Jo. Talks in question format, but you get used to it in the end.'

'I tell you what,' Andy said, and I would swear he hadn't listened to a word I'd been saying. 'I tell you what. I can see you're tired after the flight and everything. I won't come in, I'll let you have a kip and see you at sevenish. Jenny and Paul will bring you to where we're going, it's a bit of a surprise, to cheer you up. You know, after your disappointment.'

I wasn't sure I was in the mood for a surprise, but didn't want to sound ungrateful, and anyway I was tired and had to admit that the thought of a shower and a long rest with the blinds shut sounded inviting.

So after giving me a bear like hug and a kiss which I sort of wished had gone on longer, he patted me on the back and said, 'see you soon', and had gone before I knew it.

Even Jenny didn't seem to want to talk, just fetched me a cold drink and said she'd make sure I woke up in time. I'd guessed the surprise anyway. We'd often looked in at the restaurant of one of the poshest hotels in Perth and promised ourselves a slap up meal there sometime, and I knew Andy well enough to guess that first on his list of priorities was where he was going to eat that evening. Well, it suited me. Time to get my holiday back on a holiday footing and forget this obsession with my father for a while.

I unpacked my bag and fell in a heap on the bed.

When I awoke some hour and a half later I showered and, saying goodbye to the last of the smooth straight look, washed my hair then, fluffing it up with my fingers, set about deciding what to wear that evening. My new strappy little dress was hanging in the cupboard looking enticingly sexy. Whoa! Best not.

The last, indeed the only time Andy had seen me in that dress was when I'd been snapped with Nick Packer coming out of the nightclub. I chose instead a long gypsy skirt and simple white top I knew Andy would like, if and when he got round to noticing.

Briefly I wondered what he'd be wearing, then realised that unlike Nick Packer, he didn't give his clothes much attention, and didn't really need to. He always looked comfortable in whatever he had on. What was more he was comfortable in his own skin too and didn't need to keep wondering how to impress.

I clapped my hand to my head. What a fool I'd been. It must have been sheer loneliness that made me even think about Nick Packer in a romantic light. Now with Andy on the scene I knew just how wrong I'd been.

I was right about the surprise, but I didn't let on, just said how fabulous, and how it was where I'd always wanted to go for a meal.

The first person I glimpsed through the double doors as we made our way into the foyer of the hotel, was a dark haired girl with a slash of red lipstick. 'Good gracious,' I said. 'It can't be, what a coincidence . . . ' But Natasha, for I was sure it was Natasha, turned away as though she didn't want to be recognised.

'What's up?' asked Andy.

'Nothing, I thought I saw someone I knew.' Feeling hurt and with a forced smile, I didn't look Natasha's way again, but followed Andy, Jenny and Paul through to a private room.

Hold on! A private room?

'What's all this about?'

'Shh,' said Andy. 'I told you it's a surprise.'

A table had been prepared. A table with six places.

At my elbow a waitress offered a tray

of champagne. Champagne? For me? I took one quickly, in case they discovered their mistake.

'What's going on?' I asked again. Then the question died on my lips because a smiling Natasha walked through the door and all at once I knew who the man in Linda's photograph reminded me of. Not the original old photo of my dad, so much, as a real flesh and blood person — Natasha. All of a sudden I began to feel really weird. Because nothing made sense.

I reached for Andy's hand. 'I don't understand,' I said. 'What is this?'

Natasha walked towards me with both hands outstretched. 'Hi, Caro,' she said, as though she'd been my best friend forever.

'Hi,' I answered as though I'd been expecting all this to happen.

'You must be Andy?'

'Sorry,' I said belatedly remembering my manners. 'This is my boyfriend from London. Andy this is Natasha . . . Sorry, I don't know your surname

. . . Anyway, we met at Margaret River and well, that's it really.'

'Ah but you never told me your name either. Not your full name. And you never told me why you came to Australia, did you?'

A fluttery feeling was starting in the pit of my stomach. Natasha knew something.

'I need to sit down,' I said.

Looking as though he'd swallowed a couple of bowls full of cream, Andy found me a spindly legged chair and sat me down on it.

'There's someone else we want you to meet,' he said.

14

The room had gone quiet. My eyes flew towards the door. A tall guy with twinkly blue eyes was standing just inside the room. Twinkly blue eyes and close cropped silvery hair. A guy with a particular liking for a flat white and wholemeal toast and jam for breakfast. A guy with a nose like Natasha's. A guy who was smiling so much I thought his face would break in two.

He took a couple more paces into the room and I stood up but found my legs weren't working. We both stopped as though we were paralysed about a yard apart.

'Hello,' he said at last. 'I guess I'm your dad.'

I can't remember what we ate that night. Can't remember the clothes people were wearing or what music was playing or whether it was hot or cold or anything in fact other than, here was my dad and that he'd been here under my nose, or under my order pad, from my second day in Perth.

'How did you find out I was looking for you?' I asked.

'I saw your photo with the guy opening the nightclub, in the paper. I only read the blurb because I recognised you as my favourite Breakie Bar waitress. Then I made the equation. I couldn't believe that you would bother to come all this way just to find someone like me!' He looked away for a moment and I could see he was feeling pretty choked.

'Well, you're my dad, why wouldn't I?'

His blue eyes stared straight into mine, not so twinkly at the moment. 'Not much of a dad, it has to be said.'

'I'll be the judge of that . . . So what did you do? Get in touch with Nick?'

He laughed. 'No, much simpler than that. Went to the Breakie Bar and asked this English bloke built like a barn door, where you were.'

'The English bloke was me,' put in Andy. 'I took you at your word and did your shift for you while you were away, saw this guy with a briefcase full of wine lists, thought he looked a bit like your old photo. Then he started asking about you and I realised it had to be him.'

I stared open mouthed, that Andy, unimaginative Andy, who thought I'd not the remotest chance of tracing my dad — had been the one to find him.

'That night,' went on Andy, 'when you phoned from Adelaide, Brad and I were in a bar together talking about how to surprise you. It was so hard for me to pretend to be sympathetic at your not getting anywhere.'

I was still confused. 'Where does Natasha come into all this?'

'She's my niece,' said Brad.

'You've got the same noses.'

'Worst luck,' said Natasha.

'Don't be cheeky!'

'All right, Uncle Bill. You're the lucky

one Caro — you got his eyes!'

Had I? Had I really? Wow, he had fabulous eyes; it was the first thing I noticed about him. But now I was even more confused. 'Bill? But your name is Brad.'

'Yep. Bradford is an old family name. I'm Bradford Williams of Bradford Wines.'

Bradford not Bradley. Bradford — as in Bradford Wines. Ah, the company Natasha worked for. The family company Natasha was part of.

'Oh, I see!' But I wasn't sure I did. 'But why then Uncle Bill?'

Natasha laughed. 'Ever heard of Bill Bradford?'

'No.'

'Well, most Australians in the music business have. Wrote a string of hits in the nineties. Didn't perform them, but they did well. Many years ago, Grandad Williams didn't want him in the music business — felt it dragged the family name down — big row. So his younger brother Greg, that's my dad, went into the family business, and Bradford Williams became Bill Bradford.'

'But surely,' I said, 'that was just as bad. Bradford Wines, that's even more well known than Brad Williams could be.'

Brad, I couldn't really think of him as Dad, looked embarrassed and pulled at his ear. 'I know. I was very childish I'm afraid. Wanted to get back at him somehow. Prove I could make a go of it but do it under a name that was so near my own, he would still worry that people might still make the connection.'

'I don't think anyone did,' I said, and told him about all the leads I'd followed up in the music world only to arrive at a blank wall at the mention of the name Brad Williams.

'I can't believe,' I went on, 'that I was sitting talking to Natasha and never asked her if she'd heard of you. She must have been the only person I met on my travels I didn't tell my story to. And how come,' I turned to Natasha, 'how come you didn't hear Nick when he gave out the name on the stage at the Wine Fest?'

Natasha looked blank. 'Must have been busy serving the punters,' she said. 'And to tell you the truth I wouldn't make a point of listening to Nick Packer. I felt a bit sorry for you sitting on your own at Margaret River. Typical of Nick to do that. Then once we started talking I really took to you and wondered what on earth you were doing with him. I'm not his biggest fan.'

'Well, I'm not either, but I have to admit the guy did try to help me . . . Anyway, it was only because I was so used to receiving something from you every birthday that I got worried and came,' I went on to Brad, partly in order to change the subject away from Nick, and partly because — yes, why hadn't he contacted me on my birthday?

'Andy explained,' said Brad. 'But I did send you a package. It had a book in it all about Australia . . . Funny enough I was thinking about getting in touch properly now you're in your twenties — but well, I promised your mother and I didn't want to rock any boats . . . Truth is, I'm a no hassle kind of guy. Never been much good at responsibilities.'

'I was wasting my time then — you're not in the music business any more?'

'Nah.' His eyes twinkled at me. 'I had a reasonable run for my money. I travelled overseas. USA, UK and Europe. Had a great time. Some of my songs did well, but youngsters are writing their own songs now and I never had much of a voice — ask your mother. I'm back in the wine trade now. Work for my brother, Natasha's dad. I represent Bradford Wines in Perth. Not quite so exciting perhaps, but I like to know where I'm going to rest my head these days.'

I took a long hard look at Mr Flat White and Wholemeal Toast then and decided that, while it was all very romantic having him as my biological father, perhaps my mother made the right decision all those years ago. I wondered what had happened to the book he'd sent me, not that it really mattered.

★   ★   ★

Although I was glad, that I'd come, that I'd found him or rather he'd found me — I knew that while we'd always keep in touch, and there would always be a soft spot in my heart for him; he could never mean so much to me as my mum and the man I thought of as Dad. The man who'd brought me up.

It was late when we finally arrived back at Jenny and Paul's. This time Andy had taken them up on their offer of a bed for the night. Jenny and Paul made a great performance of yawning and saying how exhausted they both were before disappearing to their bedroom. Still buzzing with excitement, I turned to Andy.

'What an evening, I still can't believe it,' I kept saying half way between a laugh and a sob. 'It's just so amazing. Just when I'd given up hope . . . '

A grinning Andy came and stood very close. 'It's so good to see you happy,' he said. 'I was so scared you'd be disappointed.'

'Disappointed? How could I be? He's almost exactly as I pictured. A little older, stockier, maybe with less hair. He laughs more than I expected — very charming though, don't you think? I can see why he never settled down. Probably not very good marriage material . . . But I've got myself a cousin! And she's lovely! And she's maybe going to come to London for a visit and meet Mum and everything . . . '

My voice tailed off. 'Mum, I must phone her!'

'At this time?'

I glanced at my watch. 'It'll be about five there. That'll be fine.' I fished my phone out of my bag and turned it on. I had a message to ring home. I didn't need prompting — I was already listening to the ring tone.

'Caro,' said Mum sounding excited. 'You'll never guess what. A parcel arrived this morning from Perth. It was sent printed paper rate, which always takes longer apparently, but the post-man said it had been delayed in the system . . . Caro, can you hear me? It's OK, Brad's probably still alive, so even if you can't find him — at least we know that.'

'I know, I do know that,' I wobbled because suddenly I was feeling very emotional. 'We've found him, he's — he's nice. He's alive — not dead at all, and I've got a cousin and Andy's here and everything is absolutely wonderful.'

My voice ended on a wail. I gave the phone to Andy and cried with happiness as he explained what had happened to Mum much more coherently than I could have managed. Then I managed a brief goodbye with a promise to ring her next day for a proper chat. 'Oh and give my love to Dad,' I said. 'Tell him, well you know what to tell him. He's a great dad, you know.'

'I'll tell him,' she said.

I snapped my mobile shut and collapsed against Andy. When I'd stopped snuffling and sniffing he put a finger under my chin and forced me to look up at him.

'Better?'

'Much.'

'Care to tell me about the Nick Packer thing?'

I blushed. 'I was lonely and stupid. He was well, very attractive . . . Told me I had fabulous eyes. He, well, he noticed things about me.'

'For example?'

'For example . . . ' I feverishly searched my memory. 'He loves my hair straight . . . '

Andy gave an exasperated sigh. 'I don't love your hair. Well, I do. But I love it curly, straight, up, down. I'd love it even if it all fell out. It's not the outside that counts — it's the inside. It's not your hair I love — it's you.'

We looked into each other's eyes for a

long moment. 'Is it?' I said uncertainly.

He gave a groan and pulled me tight against him. 'I missed you so much,' he said. 'I never thought it was possible to feel so lonely . . . You seemed so far away, so out of reach . . . '

'Well, I'm not now,' I prompted in case he'd forgotten that I was here in his arms and we had a lot of time to make up.

'No, not now,' agreed Andy and his mouth came down to mine.

THE END

We do hope that you have enjoyed reading this large print book.

Did you know that all of our titles are available for purchase?

We publish a wide range of high quality large print books including:
Romances, Mysteries, Classics
General Fiction
Non Fiction and Westerns

Special interest titles available in large print are:
The Little Oxford Dictionary
Music Book, Song Book
Hymn Book, Service Book

Also available from us courtesy of Oxford University Press:
Young Readers' Dictionary
(large print edition)
Young Readers' Thesaurus
(large print edition)

For further information or a free brochure, please contact us at:
Ulverscroft Large Print Books Ltd.,
The Green, Bradgate Road, Anstey,
Leicester, LE7 7FU, England.
Tel: (00 44) **0116 236 4325**
Fax: (00 44) **0116 234 0205**

FOLLOW YOUR HEART

Margaret Mounsdon

Marie Stanford's life is turned upside down when she is asked to house sit for her mysterious Aunt Angela, who has purchased a converted barn property in the Cotswolds. Nothing is as it seems . . . Who is the mysterious Jed Soames and why is he so interested in Maynard's? And can she trust Pierre Dubois, Aunt Angela's stepson? Until Marie can find the answers to these questions she dare not let herself follow her heart.

A LOVE WORTH WAITING FOR

Karen Abbott

In the lovely village of Manorbier in Pembrokeshire, Jasmine gets the opportunity to open up a teashop — her dream come true. However, disturbing events threaten her business prospects, forcing Jasmine to search her heart and discover who wants the teashop closed. Is it the controlling boyfriend she has put in the past? Or someone wanting the premises for himself . . . local artist Rhys Morgan, for instance? Jasmine has to put her heart on hold until the sinister campaign is over.

FROM THIS DAY ON

Chrissie Loveday

When Nick arrives in a small Cornish village as doctor's locum, she's not expecting the opposition that she receives — just for being female! It seems that Doctor Roskelly, once left broken-hearted, now distrusts all women equally . . . But his Aunt Dolly, reputed to be a bit of a witch, intervenes, making Nick welcome. Gradually, the patients appreciate her — but can she ever hope to heal her own boss?

A PHOENIX RISES

Valerie Holmes

Jemma Ward's dream of a happy family home with her fiancé, Luke, is shattered by his obsession to chase a dream of riches. Her self-esteem plummets further when, in a restaurant in Kuala Lumpur, Jemma must dine alone because Luke has stood her up. Resolving to break free and take control of her future, destiny intervenes when Adam Li saves her from an attacker. At her lowest point, there's only one way for her to go — and that's up!